D1474919

THE RUNAWAY

Mr Clavering, who was in the City.

Miss Simmonds, who had a cold.

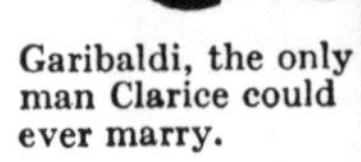

Garibaldi, the only man Clarice could ever marry.

The Policemen, who saw Olga on the roof.

Olga Leslie, ran away.

Colonel Leslie, who had led a Forlorn Hope.

Fanny, who squinted and said "Here goes!"

The respectable person who found the jewels.

Clarice Clavering, who hid Olga.

Mr Herbert, the Magistrate.

Persephone Book No 37
Published by Persephone Books Ltd 2002
Reprinted 2009

First published by Macmillan & Co. 1872, and 1936
with illustrations by Gwen Raverat.

Endpapers taken from a woodblock-printed curtain
fabric, 1936, designed and handprinted on linen by
Margaret Calkin James for the schoolroom at 'Hornbeams',
reproduced by kind permission of Elizabeth Argent

Afterwords typeset in ITC Baskerville by Keystroke,
Wolverhampton

Printed and bound in Germany by
GGP Media GmbH, Poessneck
on Munken Premium (FSC approred)

ISBN 978 1 903155 26 4

Persephone Books Ltd
59 Lamb's Conduit Street
London WC1N 3NB
020 7242 9292

www.persephonebooks.co.uk

THE RUNAWAY

by

ELIZABETH ANNA HART

****

illustrated by

GWEN RAVERAT

with new afterwords

by

ANNE HARVEY *and*

FRANCES SPALDING

PERSEPHONE BOOKS
LONDON

THE RUNAWAY

****

PREFACE

The Runaway *first appeared in* 1872, *and it was always one of our favourite books when we went to stay at our grandmother's house. Of course I cannot expect anyone else to feel such romance and excitement about it as I used to do, when I climbed into the great, curtained bed (like Miss Simmonds's bed in the picture on page* 157) *to have it read aloud to me by a sick aunt. That was in the nineties, so that I must have belonged to the second generation of children to love the book; and, since those days, my own children and many others have enjoyed the adventures of Olga and Clarice so much, that I feel that it must be worth while to have it printed again, so that it may not be lost. For I think that it is the sort of book—like* Vice Versa*—which must always be liked, because it is such fun. It is not really old-fashioned; not nearly so much so as many books which are still loved; indeed I am sure that no heroine, however modern, ever climbed trees or walls as well as Olga did. Nor is it ever pious, or proper, or sentimental; no prayers or death-beds can be found in it, and only such few tears as are very quickly dried. Neither has it that frightening quality which lurks behind the fun in* Vice Versa. *I can* *assure all parents that, though some of the pictures may appear frightening, there is nothing here to alarm the most sensitive person; for the reader always knows beforehand who the seeming ghost or burglar is, so that it is impossible to be afraid. This is hard on children, who of course like to be frightened; but parents are grown so timid nowadays, that if I did not write this, they might be afraid to read the book themselves. I should also like them to know that it is a particularly good book to read aloud.*

The Runaway *was published by Messrs Macmillan; it is by "the Author of Mrs Jerningham's Journal", whose real name was Mrs Elizabeth Anna Hart. The old book has six illustrations by J. Lawson; but though they have a certain charm, they are carelessly drawn, so that I have felt no compunction in making new illustrations. I have copied Clarice's dress from the old pictures. I have somewhat shortened the first five pages of the original book, and have omitted a second verse of the song at the end of Chapter III, but I have made no other alterations at all. I am sorry to say that historical research leads me to believe that Clarice did not marry Garibaldi after all.*

G. RAVERAT

HARLTON
August 1936

Chapter I

Clarice Clavering—young, ardent, and happy—strolled alone, by twilight, among the shrubberies in her father's garden.

"Oh, the dullness of life!" cried the young philosopher, "will lesson-time never come to an end? Oh that I might get up, read, play, walk—do everything just when I like, and not at all unless I like it! How delightful to lie in bed a whole day only because I do not choose to get up! Oh that something would happen! Oh that I had something great to live for! If I had but been so lucky as to be born in the days of the Charleses, when civil war raged through the land, and even a girl of fifteen could be in great dangers, and perform heroic deeds! but now I don't believe that there is the *slightest hope* of a revolution. It is so *hard* to think that there were very likely cavaliers who did not value their privileges, whilst *I* would give all I have in the world to have been one. Albert Lee!—only fancy—to have been Albert Lee!—to have taken that leap!—to have lived but to show my devotion to my king; and if Papa was like Sir Henry Lee, *how* I would love him! I would not a bit mind his going into passions *then*, if they were Sir Henry Lee sort of passions—not just crossnesses and strictnesses, like modern gentlemen; but everything was beautiful in those days—even men's dresses, which are so hideous now! as if a man *could* be as heroic in a chimney-pot hat, as in a delicious broad-brimmed black velvet with a magnificent plume of white feathers! Oh that I had been born a knight and a hero, in the days when knighthood was a glory, not a shame, and when heroic deeds were the daily food of happy men and women."

Thus soliloquised Clarice; and as she had just been reading *Woodstock* for the first time, her enthusiasm was not unnatural. The only daughter of a widowed merchant—who assiduously carried on his lucrative business, and would have been very much confounded had he known that his little daughter compared him disadvantageously with Sir Henry Lee—Clarice had spent her childhood in a charming home, at a convenient (railway) distance from the city, where her father repaired every morning, returning to a late dinner. Clarice had no mother and no sisters; her only brother had just entered College, and her daily companion was Miss Simmonds, her governess—an excellent, sensible woman, but one whom it was easier to respect than to love, as she had few original ideas, no fancies, a reserved manner, and a well-regulated mind. Her system of education was good; and in future years Clarice may look back and recognise how much she owed her; but at present her principal cause for feeling grateful to her is, that she occasionally reads aloud a Waverley novel, and permits her to spend some of her leisure moments over Bowdler's *Shakespeare* and Scott's poems. Now she had been listening to the pages of *Woodstock* with breathless delight, and to hide a king seemed to her the highest possible summit of earthly happiness. "Not that one could expect such a thing as *that*," she frankly admitted; for, after all, she was a sensible girl; "but if *any* thing would happen—if only *any* thing would happen!"

As Clarice made her lamentation, she had strolled from the shrubberies into a little thicket of which she was very fond, where, by the side of the winding walk, hazel, laurels, ferns, fox-gloves, and furze, all grew together in a mass.

Presently she saw a tangled part of this brush-wood moving in an odd sort of way, as if there was some animal inside it. She stood still astonished, to watch what would happen next, and what *did* happen took her breath away.

A head slowly and cautiously protruded itself from among the bushes—a head covered with such short, crisp golden curls that for a moment she thought it must belong to a young and handsome boy, but the sweet little fair face was too entirely feminine, and with a push, a scramble, a jump, and almost a fall, a body followed the head, and a girl of about her own age, or perhaps younger, stood opposite to her, panting, blushing, laughing a little, and then putting her finger on her lips and saying—"Hush! hide me; please hide me; hush!"

"My goodness!" cried Clarice. "What is it?"

"It's me!" said the girl, naturally ungrammatical at such a moment. "Oh do hide me; you will, won't you? Oh, please do!"

"Hide you?" repeated the bewildered Clarice. "From whom? where? why?"

"I've run away," said the pretty little stranger. "And now I don't in the least know what to do with myself; but of course I must be hidden—anybody would see *that*; and of course it's you must hide me since I've got here."

"But where can I hide you?" asked Clarice, almost stunned with surprise.

"Anywhere almost; I'm not big. The pantry might do, only I suppose there's a butler; and the store-room wouldn't be safe from the housekeeper; and I don't like dirt, so the coal-hole is out of the question. Isn't there a closet under the stairs?"

"Under the stairs!" sighed Clarice, speaking like one in a dream. "No, there isn't."

"Then in your own room; you must have a wardrobe—a hanging press—something!" cried the girl quickly.

"Oh yes!" said Clarice. "There's a *large* closet in my room; it runs all along in the recess of the wall, and only stops at the fire-place or chimney."

"Why did not you mention that at once?" said the stranger almost sharply; "of course that's the very place—that's where you must hide me."

"But why am I to hide you at all?" asked Clarice, beginning to recover from the stupifying effects of sudden astonishment.

"Why, because I've run away!" replied the girl simply. "Did not I tell you so?—I thought I had."

"But *why* did you run away?"

"I was so unhappy, dear! and then I was growing naughty—Oh! so frightfully naughty! One ought to bear unhappiness, you know; only I can't—some people can, and *if* you can you ought—but naughtiness! that's quite another thing; and so, as I was both unhappy and naughty, and as I can't bear the one, and ought not to bear the other, what *could* I do but run away?"

Her fair, joyful face grew very pitiful in its expression as she spoke; her rosy cheek paled a little, and big tears gathered in her pretty blue eyes.

"But what would be the use of my hiding you?"

asked Clarice; "it would be for such a very little time that it could be done—had not you better go on wherever you are going at once?"

"But I'm going nowhere," said the fair little stranger; "and since I've run away I KNOW I ought to hide—everybody does—and it's very hard if *I* must not. And I don't know what I shall do; you looked so good and kind as I peeped at you through the fern leaves, and now I'm afraid you're as cruel as all the other girls."

And she hid her face in her two hands, and began to cry.

"Oh, don't cry!" said Clarice; "I'll help you if I possibly can; only, I don't know how to get you into the house, or what I shall do with you when you're hidden."

"But you need not do anything with me *then*," cried the girl, with sudden hope; "it will all be *done* then—you'll only have to feed me. Oh, my dear, I am so hungry!" and she laughed a little.

"Do tell me," said Clarice, "where you ran away from?"

The girl came close up to her, and whispered in her ear, "From school—such a horrid strict school. I *could not* live there, I'd been so happy all my life among the mountains; and then they shut me up in a jail they called a seminary for young ladies—

ugh! and such young ladies, they LAUGHED at me! and they smuggled books into their rooms not right for us girls to read, and talked in a bad way—so silly and not at all nice—and sent me to Coventry because I would not do the same; and I had shockingly hard lessons to learn *all* day, and I was not allowed to run or to hop, not *at all*; and we were made to walk two and two, and to say dates (do you ever say dates?), and to wear backboards; and there were forty-seven people in the house, reckoning everybody from the mistress down to the knife-and-shoe-boy, and not one of them loved me, no, not the least little bit in the world, so that altogether I could not bear it, and so I ran away. Now, I've told you everything, will you hide me? Oh, please do!"

A strange feeling of delight was by this time stealing over Clarice. This girl was a heroine who had escaped from imprisonment and temptation, and come to her for help; it would have been better of course, if she had been a princess, but still it was an adventure, a real adventure, and made her heart beat fast. Something *had* happened! and just when she was in despair at the darkness of her life; yes, she would certainly help this pretty, innocent, heroic creature. She would hide her in the closet of her room, if she possibly could. It would be very difficult; how could she ever get her into the house, and upstairs, without being discovered? but, of course, adventures always *were* difficult, it was the difficulty that constituted the adventure; common life, adventureless life was easy enough, and that very easiness was what made it so dull. What merit was there in helping a suffering fellow-creature if you were not willing in some measure to sacrifice yourself? So she turned to this suffering fellow-creature, who stood looking as fair as a lily, and sparkling and beaming like a star, and taking hold of her hand, said quite solemnly, "I *will* hide you—somehow or other I will get you into my room, and hide you in the closet there."

The girl clapped her hands and laughed softly. "All right!" cried she, "and then you'll feed me without much begging, won't you? I shan't have to explain and beg like this for everything I want, shall I? I do so hate explaining—don't you?"

"I shall certainly feed you," replied Clarice very

seriously; "that *must* be a right thing to do, for nobody ought to be starved."

"Such food as we had at school!" said the suffering fellow-creature; "starving itself would be almost better than *that.* When she *said* the suet pudding had plums in it, you'd find half-a-dozen black-beetles' babies scattered through it, which you had to make believe were Smyrna currants."

"Black-beetles' babies!"

"Yes, indeed; they were little, little things, smaller than any possible beetles you know, so they *must* have been their babies, for they were as dry as sticks, and cracked in your teeth *just* like beetles."

"And were they really put into the puddings?"

"Yes; and the soup was fat, boiled in the tea that was left at breakfast, to give it a colour; and we never had anything but dog's meat—I'm quite sure we hadn't—and always from deformed animals with wrong bones, not the *least* like any bones you see anywhere else. The girls used to say shocking things about it; they said a girl who had been at that school died after she had left it some time—she did indeed—and the girls thought it was entirely from the bones, I mean from the sort of animals that *could* have such bones."

"I used to think I should like to go to school," said Clarice, with a little shudder.

"Oh, my dear! you never made such a mistake in your life. Nobody could like it; it's a horrid unhappy, wicked place; the Queen ought to put it down—she really ought—or Government or Parliament or whoever it is that *does* put things down. There *is* somebody, isn't there, who does?"

"I don't think we've any time for trifling conversation," said Clarice; "the great thing is how are we to get you into the house without being seen." She looked at her watch. "It's now or never," said she; "Papa is at dinner, Miss Simmonds is resting in her own room—she always is at this time, and the servants are all at tea. Now, then, I'll tell you what we'll do;—you go in among those shrubs, and I'll keep on the path; let me be well in advance of you, and you creep and crouch among the shrubs, but follow on, as I go; and then, if there's any danger I'll begin to sing, and as long as I keep singing you go down on your knees and hide, and when I stop then you come on again after me—do you understand?"

"Oh, perfectly; what a general you are! I'm sure your Papa must be in the army like mine; these are regular military manœuvres; just what they do when they lead a forlorn hope, or besiege a fort. My Papa has led a forlorn hope; has yours?"

"No, poor Papa, never!" said Clarice, with a

feeling of shame for her father which that worthy gentleman would not have felt for himself; "he's not in the army—I wish he was—but it's too late now; it requires so much resolution to *begin* that sort of thing late in life. And I'm sure nothing would persuade Papa to do it."

"My Papa has immense resolution," said the other.

"Yes; I dare say he has," replied Clarice sighing; "but then, you seem such a lucky girl altogether; few girls are like you, you know; they are kept safe in quiet homes, and have not a chance of running away, or anything of that sort."

"Now, I'm going in among the bushes," said the lucky one. "I do hope there'll be some danger, and that you'll begin to sing; it will be charming having to go down on all fours."

They began carrying out Clarice's military manœuvre, but the escaped heroine chuckled so joyously among the shrubs and bushes, that Clarice, in an agony lest she should betray herself, entreated her to be quiet, quite sternly. Presently Clarice saw the gardener approaching them along the wide gravel walk which they had now entered from the glade, and she immediately began to sing in her clear young voice:

> Life comes without consent,
> Life leaves us just the same;
> None knowing why it went,
> None knowing why it came.
>
> I live because I must,
> I never willed it so,
> And I shall turn to dust
> Whether I like or no!

Then the song suddenly ceased, for the gardener had turned aside along another path, and the coast was clear for the moment; so the forlorn hope continued to proceed for some time in silence, though the concealed soldier occasionally made such a rustling, scrambling noise, among the bushes, that the leader was obliged to check her with a warning hush-h.

But Clarice gave a little start of horror when she saw Miss Simmonds herself come out of the glass door that led from the house to the garden, and walk towards her with staid, measured steps. Instantly the song began again, and a great flopping sound among the bushes was the consequence:

Youth is a very sweet,
Tho' an unbidden guest;
Youth is so very fleet,
Vanishing ere possest.
It comes without a call
Just as the breezes blow,
And it will leave us all,
Whether we like or no.

"My dear Clarice," said her governess, "I have just come out to get a breath of air—the evening is really sultry, but I did not know you were in the garden. You look flushed, my love—are you quite well?"

"Yes, I am quite well," said Clarice very hurriedly; and then went on singing in a great fright, because it had been agreed that if she stopped, her companion was to come on and consider that there was no danger,

Why should life come to us
Without a yea or nay?

"You sang that E out of tune, my love," said the governess.

Why should life leave us thus
When we would have it stay?

"I don't like that song, Clarice."

When all delights are gone,
As all delights will go,
Must I keep living on
Whether I like or no?

"My dear, that song requires another verse to make it a moral. I wish you would not sing it; for though the tune is very pretty, I don't like the words."

"Miss Simmonds!" cried Clarice in despair; "Jenkins went down just now towards the strawberry beds, and we have never told him about the Camellias, and he will attend to you so much better than to me—*won't* you go and talk to him now?"

She spoke with desperate rapidity, running her words into each other.

"Certainly, my dear, I will," replied Miss Simmonds very slowly; "won't you come too?"

"No, no, no!" cried Clarice; "I am tired and must go in."

And then, in a violent hurry, she began another song,

All day long the empty skies
Must be longing for the stars,
For the cruel sun did rise
Closing up their prison bars.

"I wish, Clarice, you would attend to me, and not keep on singing—and you hurry so—that ought to be sung in a slow, undulating way."

Oh, the empty skies are dull,
Not a solitary star;
But at night how beautiful,
And how full of them they are.

"You don't undulate in the least," said Miss Simmonds; "there is no good in singing a song of that sort unless you undulate." With which words she walked leisurely away down the side-path in search of Jenkins the gardener.

Clarice made an eager, silent sign of encouragement to the bushes, and then without further molestation proceeded on her way towards the glass door through which her governess had made her appearance. She went softly into the house, ran up-stairs, and into her bedroom, looking cautiously round her all the time. Satisfied with the result of this reconnoitre, she descended again, and clasping her companion's hand in her's, whispered in her ears, "Come as quickly and as quietly as possible."

Hand-in-hand the two young creatures rushed into the house and up the staircase, Clarice very gravely, and with an animated expression in her face, the other laughing under her breath so much that the laughter almost retarded her steps.

"What a girl you are for laughing!" cried Clarice, when, the bed-chamber reached and the door locked, they stood facing each other, and feeling safe but excited.

"Yes," said she apologetically; "I know I am—it's a great pity, but I can't help it—and then, you know, I'm not grown up yet. I don't mean to laugh *at all* when I am, so I'm getting it all over now."

"How old are you?" asked Clarice.

"I'm more than thirteen, but I'm not fourteen yet. I'm *sure* you're fifteen—now, are not you?"

"Yes, I was fifteen the first of this month—but will you tell me what your name is?"

"Olga!"

"Olga!" repeated Clarice, quite appalled. "Olga! well, you *are* a lucky girl—what a name! and *really* to have it, in these days—why, it did not seem possible that anybody could have such a name as *that*, except, perhaps, a Danish princess."

"Mama *is* a Dane," replied Olga, "and I am called after her, and I am just like her they say, only I know I'm not, for she is like an angel, and I'm an every-day girl."

"Why don't you go to your mother, then?" asked Clarice abruptly.

"Why, don't you know she's in India?—oh, no, of course you don't—it seems so odd to me always, how people don't know about one without being told, but they never do. I'm sure birds and animals know all about each other when they meet; don't you think they do? I've noticed it often, in birds especially. But Papa is colonel of a regiment, and he and Mama are both in India, and I live with dear Grandmama in a Scotch castle—only I don't, because they sent me to school."

"You live in a Scotch castle!" repeated Clarice in quiet, subdued accents, as of one who, having acknowledged her companion to be the most fortunate of girlkind, could now be surprised at nothing.

At that moment a loud bell rang.

"That is for my tea with Papa," said Clarice.

"Hide me! hide me!" cried Olga.

Clarice opened the cupboard. It was nearly two feet wide and about eight long, so that the end furthest from the door, which was not in the middle, but at the end of the side, thus, ⌐¬ ⌐ was quite concealed from view, and there was no window in the closet; there were hooks along the wall, with dresses and cloaks hanging on them, and there were a few books, some portfolios of music and drawings, and a box or two on the floor.

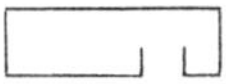

Olga ran, laughing, in.

"Here's the key," said Clarice. "Shall I lock you in, or will you have it and lock yourself in—which? be quick now, for I must not keep Papa waiting!"

"Give it me then—I'll lock myself in. Oh, how dark, dear—it *is* dark!"

"I'll come back the very minute I can, and bring some bread and butter; but, *mind* you keep as quiet as a mouse, or, rather, much quieter than any mouse, for Ann will be in doing the room for the night. You *must* not laugh."

"I never laugh in the dark," said Olga solemnly. "I hate it so. Oh dear me! I do like running away, but I find I don't like being hidden."

Chapter II

Mr Clavering liked his little daughter to pour out his tea for him; and though there was not much confidential communication between the city man and the enthusiastic girl, this tête-à-tête at the end of his busy day refreshed him, as cool twilight refreshes the earth after sultry noon.

Miss Simmonds wisely fell into the arrangement, and drank her own tea earlier in the schoolroom. By this means she secured to herself the free enjoyment of the evening hours—always a boon to a hard-working, conscientious governess—and soon after tea she was accustomed to make her appearance down stairs. Then Mr Clavering assembled his household and read prayers. After which the ladies retired to their rooms, and the gentleman sat up—perhaps into the small hours—reading, writing, dozing, and smoking.

On this particular evening poor Clarice was very distrait in her manner—so much so as to draw her father's attention, though he was by no means a particularly observant man.

"My dear! what is the matter?" asked he; "you are putting the sugar into the teapot, and the tea into the slop-basin. Are you not feeling well?"

Clarice was just on the point of admitting that she was not feeling very well, as the easiest way of getting out of the difficulty, but before the words had passed her lips, a feeling of terror seized her as she reflected that they would not be the truth. "I must be exceedingly careful," she thought to herself; "I am practising a great concealment. It is difficult to be perfectly true in word and deed when you are concealing anything; but I *must* be true. If I equivocate, or tell nasty little lies, I at once make the concealment wrong. But I am not *quite* sure whether sometimes it may not be necessary and right to tell one big lie and have done with it—not for me *now*, but whether sometimes it might not—to save the king's life, perhaps."

"Papa!" said she suddenly out loud, "if you were hiding the king—"

"There *is* no king, Clarice!" replied her father mildly.

"No, I know there is not; but that does not make a bit of difference. However, to please you I'll *put* it differently;—if you were hiding the Prince of Wales—"

"It does not please me in the least, my dear; I think it sounds like great nonsense."

"But it is not nonsense," cried she impatiently. "Quite the contrary—it is sense—it is a question in morals. I almost believe it is metaphysics. But suppose you were hiding the Prince of Wales—let us say behind the fire-place—"

"I couldn't hide him behind the fire-place," replied her father.

"Oh yes, you could! in old houses you could; there are little chambers behind the fire-places in old houses, on purpose for concealment."

"And how do you get at them?"

"I don't know. It doesn't signify. I think part of the back slips aside, and then you get your hand in and move something, and it all comes away; but it is not of the slightest consequence where you are hiding him. It may be behind the fire-place, or in a trap-door, or—"

"Not *in* a trap-door, my love," replied Mr Clavering calmly; "there would not be room."

"Oh Papa, how tiresome you are! All that has nothing to do with the question."

"I did not know there *was* a question."

"No, of course you didn't; because you *will* interrupt. If you will only just let me go on and say what I want to say. Suppose you are hiding the Prince of Wales (she spoke in quite a weary voice, as if worn-out by her father's behaviour)—and a traitor came in and asked if he was there, what would you do?"

"I should call a policeman, and have the traitor (if he was labelled traitor, so that there was no doubt about him) marched off to the station-house."

"Well, yes!" continued she after a moment's silence, "you might do that under particular circumstances; but suppose there were not the circumstances, so that you could not do it. My case is this—you must either tell a falsehood and save the Prince's life, or tell the truth and sacrifice it. Now, what would you do?"

"I should tell the falsehood, my dear, if I knew the traitor was really going to murder the Prince, or to dethrone his family."

"I suppose it *would* be right," said she, thoughtfully; "but, then, that is such an extreme case; there is the divine right of kings, of course, and loyalty, and every feeling, and every principle too, to make one do it; but suppose it wasn't the king. Oh, I beg your pardon—you can't imagine cases—supposing it wasn't the Prince, I mean, but a friend; or not even a friend—anybody—a foot-boy, perhaps—what would you do then?"

"And you don't call that imagining cases? I wonder what it is then. Well, if it was a friend, it would depend on a great many things—what the danger was I saved him from, and who the person was who came after him. I might consider myself justified in saying what was not true, but I should not like it, and I should be slow to do it. As to the foot-boy, I will venture to say I would not tell a lie about the foot-boy; but then, the fact is, I wouldn't conceal the foot-boy at all."

"That would be very unjust, Papa."

"Perhaps it would, Clarice; but I'm pretty sure

I should tell the foot-boy to go about his business in the first instance."

"Well, Papa, but it is very odd and puzzling that there should be cases in which it is right to tell a lie, and it is very difficult to draw the line, and to know exactly where they begin."

"I'll tell you what, my dear, if I were you I wouldn't trouble my head about it. There *can* be no case in which it would be right for a child like you to tell a falsehood, and, in after life, it is highly improbable that such a case should ever occur in your experience. As a general rule it is safe to stick to the maxim, 'Tell truth and shame the Devil.' If you keep to the spirit of truth in everything, not only to the letter, you won't blunt your perceptions, but will keep them delicate and fine, and you may then trust to your own conscience to preserve you *truthful*, even if you should ever be compelled by circumstances to save a life by telling a murderer a falsehood."

"Thank you, Papa; I'm sure you are right—I like to hear you talk so. Oh, what a pity it is you are a merchant!"

"Good gracious, Clarice! Why?"

"Oh, never mind! you wouldn't understand. Papa, *wouldn't* you like to be a soldier? Don't quite old people sometimes go into the army? If you did something very desperate and daring you might have a high command given you at once, mightn't you?"

"No, my dear, I shouldn't like to be a soldier at all; and if I tried to do anything desperate or daring, I'm sure I should be very much frightened, and run away in the middle of it."

"Oh Papa, Papa! please don't say such things; they make me feel so small and miserable."

"My dear Clarice! for a sensible, clever girl, which you undoubtedly are, you are a great little goose." Then Clarice poured out her father's second cup of tea in silence, and her own too, and for some minutes not a word was said; but she was only re-collecting her forces, and soon began again.

"It may not be possible for it to be right for a child like me ever to tell a falsehood," said she, "but it may sometimes be unavoidable that she should practise a concealment."

"She'd much better practise a sonata."

"Don't laugh, Papa; I am quite in earnest."

"But you use such odd phrases, my dear. What do you mean by practising a concealment?"

"Having some great things that it is a duty to conceal."

"Stuff and nonsense!"

"No, Papa, it is not stuff and nonsense. Remember, I don't consider it my duty never to conceal anything. I don't make you a promise not to have concealments."

"I'm sure I never thought of asking for such a promise."

"No! but I want you clearly to understand, and then I shall never feel as if I was deceiving you."

"Look here, Clarice! you may have any trumpery concealments from me that you like while you are a child—I'm not a man to pry into nonsense like that—but you won't be a child long; in another year or two you'll be a woman; and, by George, if you conceal any of your love affairs from me, then, I'll know the reason why!"

"Love affairs!" cried Clarice with the utmost disdain; "no, Papa, you need not be afraid of *that*—I shall never have any love affairs—I shall never marry."

"Oh you won't, won't you? and, pray, why not?"

"Because," replied she very seriously, "I don't like the men of the present day."

Mr Clavering burst out laughing.

"Do you and Miss Simmonds talk all this sort of stuff together?" asked he.

"Never! how could we? She doesn't understand things. *You* almost do understand things, Papa. I think you would quite if—"

"If what, Clarice?"

"If you would give up going into the city."

"And lead a forlorn hope instead, I suppose."

Clarice blushed violently.

"Oh Papa, did you overhear?—do you know?"

She stopped in great excitement and embarrassment, with her eyes fixed entreatingly on her father's face.

"I overheard nothing, Clarice—I only spoke at random. Have you been plotting for me to lead a forlorn hope, then? It's a great pity you're not Garibaldi's daughter."

"Papa, don't make me discontented. I *can't* be his daughter; but you talk about marrying, and I would marry Garibaldi to-morrow if he asked me, and he is the only man in the world I ever would."

"Forewarned, forearmed, Clarice! I'm glad you told me. I decidedly object to my future son-in-law, and shall do my best to prevent the match."

Here, Miss Simmonds making her appearance, the conversation dropped. The bell was rung, the servants assembled, prayers were read, and Good-nights exchanged.

Clarice went on tiptoe up-stairs to her own

room, as if caution and secrecy must begin at once. She closed the door and locked it, then put her candle on the table, and going quickly to the closet, whispered through the keyhole, "Olga, Olga, it is I; open the door!"

There was no answer, and no sound inside the closet. She spoke louder, but the silence was the same. Clarice wrung her hands in great distress. "She is asleep; she will be starved; she will be smothered; she will die—locked in there by herself all the night long." Then she pushed against the door, and to her amazement it yielded to her touch and opened. It was not locked! She seized her candle and entered the closet, holding the light in advance of her towards the distant end. The closet was empty!

Clarice came back into the room very softly, looking pale and scared. She put her candle down, and then seated herself and began to think. Olga was gone; but had she ever been there? Had it all really happened? or was it a dream, a vision, a delusion? Was she going mad, and should she take to dreaming dreams and seeing visions? She pressed her hands against her forehead and shuddered at the thought. No, that was all nonsense, and it was mere weakness to indulge in such fancies. She *had* met her in the garden; she *had* brought her home, singing as she went to warn her against dangers; she *had* hidden her in that closet, and Olga's pathetic entreaty—"Hide me, Oh, please hide me!" still rung in her ears. Olga had escaped, had run away again, and this delightful, exciting, dangerous, tormenting, difficult adventure had come to an ignominious end.

Then she went to the windows and examined them, but they were still fastened on the inside. How had she got out? Through the door, and probably had left the house while everyone was at prayers, so that she had slipped away unobserved.

"So that is over," said she to herself in a depressed way, "and there is nothing more to expect now."

She took a roll of bread and sundry cakes, with which she had filled her pockets before coming upstairs, and laid them on the table, and then, with the air and movements of one who had recently undergone some great fatigue, she began slowly and wearily to undress. She was in her dressing-gown, and brushing her hair when she went up to the side of the bed to let down the curtain, but in the same moment that she did this, she gave a great jump and a scream. On her pillow lay a head covered with crisp, shining golden curls, a little fair face nestled there, with closed eyes and rosy lips slightly parted.

Olga had taken possession of her bed, and was sleeping so soundly that no noise Clarice had made since she entered the room had reached her brain through the closed portals of the senses.

But Clarice's scream woke her in a moment. She opened her blue eyes, and said, "Where *can* I be?"

Then Clarice, half-angry and half-frightened, took hold of her small white shoulders, shook her slightly, and said, "How dare you get into my bed!"

Olga laughed a little and nestled herself down on the pillow. "What could I do?" she cried. "I was so tired—so tired, and I had only the bare boards to crouch on. I heard your Ann go away, and then I took off some of my dusty, dusty clothes, and I was obliged to get into *your* bed, my dear, because there was no other. Oh, do let me go to sleep again! Get in quick, I'll make room for you;—I will indeed," she added, as if she was proposing to do rather a meritorious thing.

"Yes," said Clarice discontentedly; "but I am not at all sleepy, and there is so much I want to hear. I must know a great deal more about you if I am to keep you, and it was so very, *very* imprudent of you to leave that safe cupboard. Suppose—only just suppose—anybody had come in and found you here!"

"It would have been such fun!" cried Olga, laughing. "They'd have thought you had moulted yellow, and got rid of all your pretty brown feathers;" and she took hold of one of Clarice's long dark curls, and gave it a little twitch, with a friendly, roguish look in her eyes.

"I brought you a great deal to eat," answered Clarice in an injured tone.

Olga sat up in the bed and clapped her hands.

"Oh, you did, you did, you good, dear brown

bird! give it me, give it me—I am dying with hunger; I could eat those baby beetles, and the very dog's meat itself, with a relish now. I really believe I could."

Then she took the roll and the cakes, and ate them in a pretty dainty way—more like a delicate fairy than a ravenous mortal girl.

"Olga!" said Clarice, gravely, "I must have some serious talk with you. What is your other name?"

"Leslie; Papa is Colonel Leslie, one of the Scotch Leslies, you know. Oh, if you could see him in Highland costume, with a little dagger in his sandled knee!"

Clarice sighed, and thought regretfully of *her* father's pepper-and-salt trousers.

"And where were you at school?"

"At York, dear."

"At York! Oh, Olga! you don't mean to say that you ran away all the way from York, here."

"Yes, I did indeed—in a railway."

"Oh, in a railway!"

"Yes; I put on the housemaid's cloak and

bonnet; and in the very middle of the night, when everybody was fast asleep, I got out of the window on to the top of the porch, and then I scampered down the trellis like a cat, and walked off by moonlight a mile and a half to the station—we are not *in* York, you know, only in a suburb—and there

I got a ticket, and a train was just coming up—was not that lucky?—and so off I came to you, who were waiting for me among the furze blossoms. Oh, what is your name? I don't know a bit what your name is, my dear brown bird!"

"My name is Clarice," said the brown bird, smiling, and kissing the joyous little creature; "but tell me, how could a child like you have money enough for such a journey?"

"I stole it, dear Clarice!" answered she, with a roguish look.

Clarice drew back shocked. "Oh no! don't say that; I hope not; you didn't really, did you?"

"Oh no, I did not—Leslies are not thieves—that was a lie!" cried Olga, with such a burst of chuckling laughter, that Clarice, unable to resist the infection, laughed too.

"Grandmama, bless her! had sent me ten pounds to give to Mrs Jennings to buy me some books and clothes. Mrs Jennings said it was a most irregular proceeding, as all money ought to be sent to her direct, but Grandmama *is* irregular—I like old people to be irregular, don't you?"

"Yes, of course I do," sighed Clarice, "everybody must; but then they so seldom are."

"So I took a third-class ticket, and I've plenty of money left. The only unlucky thing is that the train was going just the wrong way. I've come to one end of England when I meant to go to the other end of Scotland—however, after all, that's only a trifle."

"Did you mean to go to your Grandmama?"

"No! because she's not at home at present, and Aunt Jessie's at the castle, and Aunt Jessie won't do at all—not at all"; and she shook her head emphatically.

"*She* is awfully regular, and everything else you can think of that an aunt shouldn't be. She'd tell me to keep my drawers tidy, and darn my stockings, and read fifty pages of a good book every day out of my own head, *besides* my lessons! She's a sort of person that one wonders why she ever was born, and if she got born by accident, one wonders why she's let live."

"Then what did you mean to do?"

"I meant to hang about at Inns like a man!" cried Olga with a burst of laughter, "till Aunt Jessie went away and Grandmama came back, and then to assault Grandmama with the news of how unhappy I was, and how she must never, never, never, never, *never* send me back to that horrid jail again."

"And where is your Grandmama now?"

"Ah! that I don't know. She's gone on a visit somewhere, but I've no notion where, only I'm afraid she's going to stay a long time. Oh, Clarice! don't you think it would be nice for me to get a blue jacket, and a striped shirt, and a pair of wide white trousers, and a smart little oilskin hat, and go to sea, and be a real sailor-boy?"

"No, indeed, I don't think it would be at all nice."

"If I did, I would always keep a boy; I'd never come home and be a girl again. It must be so sweet to be a boy! boys have no excuse for ever doing wrong; they ought to be so thankful for being what they are."

"I don't know," replied Clarice doubtfully.

"I don't like modern boys. Pages now—there is a good deal to be said for them—but modern boys—no, Olga, they are not worth much."

"Well, in my opinion, men and women are a mistake—there ought only to be boys and girls. Just think, what a world it would be if boys and girls never grew up!"

But Clarice shook her head.

"It would not do," she said; "it would not do at all—boys and girls can do so little. There would only be high aspirations—there would be no fulfilment."

Olga opened her blue eyes wide, and stared at her. "I don't know what you are talking about," said she; "it sounds like gibberish."

"Never mind," replied Clarice; "we all speak gibberish to others, I think, when we say what we really feel."

"*I* feel very sleepy," said Olga, "but that is not gibberish, is it?"

"No," said Clarice smiling, "because I am getting sleepy too; when people feel alike they don't talk gibberish."

"Well then, come into bed, and let us go to sleep as fast as ever we can."

"But you'll have to get up quite early in the morning, and hide in that closet before Ann calls me; and I shall have to tumble the bed about, for fear she should see two people have slept in it."

"All right," said Olga.

"Yes; but I must ask you a question or two first," continued Clarice, as she finished undressing, and crept into bed; "your Papa and Mama are in India, you say?"

"Yes, and they came home to see us all two years ago, and they are coming again this year, and they said I was to get accomplished; so soon as I was thirteen I was to go to school and get accomplished there."

"Then you did not learn much at the Castle?"

"Indeed I did, though—plenty. Grandmama plays so well; and she taught me music and French, and the old minister taught me arithmetic and geography, and all that English rubbish; and I could ride faster, walk farther, dance longer, and catch more fish than any other girl in the country."

"What a happy life you must have had!"

"Happy! I was as happy as a queen; but, oh Clarice! let us go to sleep now, and give me a kiss—there's a dear; nobody ever kissed me the whole time I was at school—not anybody ever once!"

Clarice kissed her heartily, and Olga returned the kiss with pretty childish caresses. Then the two girls went to sleep, as young creatures will do, however much they have to think about, and slept soundly till morning.

It was a great shock to Clarice when she heard Ann making a noise at the door, and saw the sun was climbing up the sky, while Olga still lay asleep by her side. She woke her cautiously, with many a whispered "Hush!" and "Don't speak!" and "There's somebody there!"

At last Olga's blue eyes were well opened, and the dazed look went out of them, and she was wide awake; and then, to Clarice's dismay, she began to laugh. Clarice kept her as quiet as she could, and dragged her out of bed, and across the room, and into the cupboard, and then turned the lock on her, telling her, in a whisper, to dress herself there and keep perfectly quiet. She then unlocked the door, and ran back into bed, which she tumbled about as much as she could.

"What is the meaning of this, Miss Clarice," cried angry Ann, "locking yourself in, and keeping me half-an-hour at the door? Indeed, Miss, I wasn't hired to stand outside your door, and I haven't time to waste that way, either."

"I can't help it, Ann," replied Clarice, coldly; "I shall lock my door if I like; and I can't help it if I don't wake directly."

"If you went to bed at fittin' times and seasons, Miss, it's my belief you'd wake easy; but you sit up at night reading them story-books—that's what you do; and I'll tell Miss Simmonds of you."

"You are quite at liberty to tell Miss Simmonds anything you please. Now, be so good as to open the shutters, and put down the hot water, and then go away."

Ann obeyed, muttering, in a revengeful manner, to herself all the time.

Clarice got up as soon as she was gone, said her prayers—which she had not neglected on the previous night, though we made no special mention of the fact—dressed herself, and then let Olga out. She had before this supplied her with washing apparatus, so that she was able to perform her ablutions in the privacy of the long closet.

"Now," she said, "enjoy the fresh air for a few minutes, for I must then shut you up till after breakfast, when I will bring you some food. Most fortunately this is a holiday, and Miss Simmonds is sure to spend it in her own room writing letters; so, at least, I shall be able to be with you; and if we can do nothing better we can lock ourselves up here and amuse ourselves."

Olga threw herself into her arms, and kissed her warmly, after which she consented to return into her prison, though she said mournfully, as she did so, "It is unlucky, but I *am* frightened in the dark."

Clarice ran down to breakfast, and found her father and Miss Simmonds already there. Mr Clavering was a punctual man, and few things offended him more than a want of punctuality in his daughter.

"You are late, Clarice," he said sternly. "Don't let this happen again."

Clarice could talk freely to her father, as she had done the night before, when he was in the humour for it, and he dearly loved his one girl, and, in many respects, indulged her, but he was very strict and particular in his notions, and could be exceedingly stern. She greatly feared his displeasure, and knew well that he could make it a thing to be greatly feared.

"Why did you lock your door last night?" asked Miss Simmonds.

Clarice blushed painfully. "I like locking my door," she said in a low voice.

"Did you ever do it before?" continued her governess.

"No!"

"Ann complains that you kept her outside so long while she tried to make you hear her, that she had to neglect her work."

"Don't lock your door, Clarice," said Mr Clavering; "it's a foolish habit, and I won't have it."

"It is very hard that I mayn't lock my own door," murmured Clarice, with a painful emotion, that appeared quite disproportioned to the occasion.

"Hey! what's this?" cried he, laying down his newspaper, and looking with surprise and anger at her vivid colour and rising tears; "if you can't keep your temper you had better go to your room; but, remember what I say—you are *not* to lock your door at night."

Clarice controlled herself as well as she could, swallowed down her tears, and ate her breakfast in silence.

Chapter III

When breakfast was finished, her father gone to catch the train for London, and Miss Simmonds safe in her own room, Clarice cut some slices of bread and butter, and, taking the jug of milk also in her hand, went up-stairs to Olga, feeling decidedly out of spirits. As she entered her room she heard a faint moaning sound from the closet, and, with a sensation of fear, she hastily closed the door and fastened it, saying to herself as she did so, "It is day-time—but what *shall* I do at night?" Then she unlocked the closet, and looking in, found Olga crouching on the floor, moaning softly, and with her face bathed in tears. She sprang out as the door opened, almost as a bird might fly from its cage. "Oh, I'm afraid—I am afraid!" she exclaimed.

"Poor little thing!" said Clarice, kindly caressing her; "here is some breakfast for you; you will be better when you have taken that."

Olga ate and drank with avidity, and then, drying her tears, said in an energetic manner, "Clarice, you *must* find me another hiding-place; I can't go into that black darkness again; I will hide *anywhere* else. I would rather be up the chimney, because there *is* light at the top there."

"What are you afraid of?" asked Clarice. "I don't at all mind being in the dark."

"Oh, I do! I am afraid of everything and of nothing—of ghosts, bogies, bears, live things, dead things, and myself!"

"I don't in the least know where else to put you."

"Well, don't mind now, you must stay with me a little, and then I needn't be anywhere!"

"If we could go out, it would be very nice. See what a fine day it is, and how the sun shines. I wonder whether we could manage it—it would be delicious in the glade."

"I could get out of the window quite easily,"

said Olga, leaning over the wall, "and climb down by the jessamine branches."

Clarice pulled her back. "How can you be so imprudent?" cried she; "you will be seen and discovered."

Olga pouted. "Well, but I must go out, you know, Clarice—you said so yourself, and I shall go into a consumption if I don't take regular exercise."

"Yes," said Clarice laughing; "of course you will in two days; but if we *could* get to the glade, Olga, we might spend the morning there—then I might come back to dinner, and you stay, hiding in the glade, and I could bring you something to eat afterwards."

"I must have meat," said Olga, with the air of a queen issuing her commands, "or my blood will become poor, and vegetables, or I shall have the scurvy"; and she pursed up her little mouth to keep from laughing.

"You must be content with whatever I can manage to bring," replied the other; "I will do the best I can for you, but I make no promises. If there is cold meat it will be easy; but how am I to carry out hot meat, I wonder?"

"Bees or ants can contrive *any* thing," said Olga; "what a pity it is girls are not so ingenious. I often think I should like to be an ant."

"Well, if one must be one of them, I should rather choose to be a bee," said Clarice.

"Ah! that's because you look at the matter superficially—you have not thought it out as I have—*any* body would rather be a bee if honey was not sticky, but honey *is* sticky, and there is *no* drawback to being an ant."

"What an odd girl you are," said Clarice, laughing. "I wonder if you are one of those Norwegian spirits who appear on the sea-shore after a storm, and marry the King of the country, and go on just like ladies, till some word or act dissolves the spell, and then they turn into wandering spirits again. With your name and your face, and your way of talking, I think you are more like one of them than a real girl. Are you a real girl, Olga?"

"Who knows?" cried Olga, with that expression,

at once friendly and roguish, in her eyes, that gave such an elfish look to her gold-crowned head. "And what *is* real? Is anybody real? I dare say I am just as real as other people."

"Miss Simmonds is real enough, anyhow," replied Clarice, half-smiling, half-sighing; "and I think my best plan is to go to her, and tell her I mean to take a book into the glade, and shan't be back till dinner. There is one great piece of luck—she has got a cold, so she will stay in-doors all day, and won't expect me to walk with her."

"Run, run, and be back directly!" cried Olga; "and then we will fly to the glade. There is an important reason why I ought to go there as soon as possible—I left my bag there."

"Left your bag there!"

"Yes; left it in the fern tangle, out of which I crept when you first saw me, and forgot all about it from that moment to this; my dear little travelling-bag with clothes in it, and all my money and—jewels."

"Jewels!"

"Yes, why not? But never mind that now. I want you to be quick, that we may fly away to the glade and be happy."

"But you must go into the cupboard again while I am gone."

"I won't!"

"But you must, indeed, Olga! Ann might come into my room, or Miss Simmonds might accompany me back. It's not the least safe for you to be here without me."

"I won't go into that cupboard!"

"Now, don't be obstinate; you'll spoil everything; and it is so silly to be frightened. Go in like a good girl, and I shan't be away a minute."

"I won't. I never will go into that closet again—not if I live to be a hundred and thirty-three years old. It's a shocking black place, and I'm afraid."

"What *could* happen to you?"

"I might go out—I know I might—just like a candle. It's no use talking to me; I *felt* I might when I was there. It's not dark, it's *black*, and it's all space, and a live thing there might go out any minute, just like a candle, and never be seen again, because it could be nowhere, any more than the flame of a candle is when it's gone out."

"Oh, Olga! how can you talk such nonsense? but you are not behaving well; you come here and throw yourself upon me, and expect me to take care of you and hide you, and then you refuse to go into the only place where you can be hidden. It's not fair—I think it's not at all fair."

"I hate being fair," said Olga; "it's always stupid."

"Very well," replied Clarice, coldly, "then you can do as you please—of course it's nothing to me. I shall tell Miss Simmonds I am going to the glade, and then I shan't come back, but shall go there straight, and you can stay here if you like."

"You'll find me there," said Olga, and, before Clarice could prevent her, she was out of the window, and the next instant stood on the walk beneath, for she had descended by aid of the jessamine branches nailed against the house, with an agility that took away the breath of her more sober companion.

Then she looked up, laughed, nodded her bright head up and down, kissed her hand, pointed towards the glade, and disappeared among the bushes.

Clarice paid her visit to Miss Simmonds, and then walked through the garden to the glade, wondering whether she should find the volatile Olga there. "If she has gone away, and I never see her again," thought she; should she be glad? should she be sorry? She was a great trouble to her; she kept her anxious and pre-occupied, she foresaw more difficulties every day, and yet she could not truthfully say that she wished either that she had never come, or that she would now vanish away among the tangled fern as mysteriously as she had issued out of their midst. The excitement and vivid interest which the adventure lent to her daily life made up for all the rest.

It was therefore with a feeling of blank, unmixed disappointment, that when she reached the glade she looked and wandered all about it, and found no Olga there. "She is gone," she said. "It is over—she is gone," and she repeated this many times before she could convince herself that it was true. It was strange to her, to reflect that she had never seen the girl before the previous evening, and that her life was now exactly what it had always been till half-a-day back; for at the moment it seemed to her as if she was now deprived for the first time of the principal object of that life. At last she sat down under an oak tree, and, opening her book, tried to read, and to forget that Olga had ever existed, or that she had ever seen her.

Suddenly an acorn fell on the open volume. Involuntarily Clarice looked up, throwing her head back, in order that she might see better through the leafy branches, when another acorn fell right on her nose, and gave it a pretty sharp little rap. What was it? a bird, a squirrel, or—Olga? Her heart beat quite fast as she peered eagerly up, trying to distinguish the naughty, pretty creature. But she saw no one; only she heard—what was it she heard? Oh, wonderful—in the middle of that sultry July day, out of the oak tree came the song of the cuckoo—the Spring Cuckoo, the April Cuckoo—for in the unchanging voice of the bird dwelt all the freshness of that first youth which was to supply the untired note for so many weeks to come.

Then the cuckoo ceased its chant, and other birds began, and from the cool chirp of the sparrow to the triumphant roundelay of the thrush, the songs of all the birds she knew seemed to be imprisoned in that one green canopy above her.

As suddenly as it had commenced, the concert ceased, and a joyous, chuckling, girl laugh followed, while the rustling leaves made place for a golden head and fair face,

which,
peeping out at her,
looked like the bodiless angel heads in old pictures, wanting only the wings instead of a neck to be the angel-head complete. "I can imitate animals just as well as birds," cried a gay sparkling voice, "so that they all come flocking round me, only I dare not do it here, you know, as cows and horses cannot be supposed to live in this glade."

"Come down, naughty child," said Clarice quite fondly, and down ran Olga like a squirrel, and nestled by her side.

"I have found my bag," cried she, "and only think, the mouth was open, and half the things had tumbled out, but I hope I have collected them all; and Oh, Clarice! as I was picking them up, only just fancy, I saw a man looking at me over the hedge—he was in the lane outside you know; but wasn't it rude?"

"I don't know," answered Clarice; "he must

have been surprised to see a little girl like you packing a travelling-bag in a wood."

They both laughed at this idea; but Olga said, rather seriously for her, "He was not a *nice* man—not at all a *nice* man, Clarice."

"Now, Olga," said Clarice, "I want you to attend to me quietly—we really ought to form plans, you know. I have not the least idea what you mean to do."

"I don't mean to do anything, dear!" murmured Olga, smiling sweetly.

"But about staying here or going away?"

No answer.

"Where do you want to go, Olga, and when?"

"Nowhere, dear, and not at all."

"But you can't mean to live here always—to grow up here hidden, and never seen by anyone but me?"

"I don't mean anything. I will just stay here till something turns up."

"Won't you write to your Grandmama?"

"I don't know where she is."

"But your schoolmistress will write to her?"

"Perhaps she will; and if so, something will turn up. But Grandmama won't be pleased; and I'm so afraid she'll want me to go back to school."

"But something must be done, you know, Olga."

"Yes, of course; but there's no hurry. It need not be done just yet, or by us. I'm going to wait. I took the first step. I ran away; but I needn't take all the steps, you know that wouldn't be fair. It's their turn now."

"Then you mean—"

"Just to hide here for a day or two and see what happens—it's very pleasant in this wood."

"Yes, but you don't think it pleasant in the dark closet."

"That's all stuff—why should it be a dark closet? let's get one of the stable-lamps and hang up in it."

"Well, really, Olga, that is a clever notion, I never thought of that. We might get a lantern, certainly."

"A bright, *bright* paraffin lamp, not one of your faint die-away lanterns, that just gives light enough to *see* the ghosts and the dim things moving about, but a flood of light, Clarice, to keep my spirits up."

"I don't know about that; but I'm sure we can get something to prevent you going out in the dark, you foolish child."

"You may laugh, but it's a real danger; I know it is."

Then Olga fetched her bag, and kept opening and shutting it, giving Clarice little sudden peeps of things inside—a glimpse of a bank note, a handful of sovereigns, diamonds, gold like a coiled-up necklace. Clarice exclaimed in astonishment, and Olga went off into fits of joyous laughter at her surprise.

"My jewels!" she cried; "did not I tell you I had jewels?"

"But where could a girl like you get such jewels?" demanded the wondering Clarice.

"They are part of myself," was the answer; "I was born with them. Did you not know that little Danes are born covered with jewels?"

"They are born very foolish, I think," replied Clarice sedately, "and do not get any wiser as they grow older."

At that moment the dinner bell rang.

"Oh, what a pity!" cried both the girls.

"I must go," Clarice said, "but I shall return the very minute I can, and bring you something to eat."

"Meat and vegetables," cried Olga imperiously; "don't forget."

"Now you'd better not set your heart upon vegetables, for I don't one bit think I shall be able to bring them."

"Then I shall have scurvy," said Olga in a dejected manner; "it won't be pleasant, of course, but what must be, must be."

Clarice walked quietly back to the house, and joined Miss Simmonds at the dining-table.

"I think, my dear," said that lady, "that although it *is* a holiday, you had better not be out of doors all day. You might practise your music for an hour after dinner—you generally play and sing a good deal on a holiday."

"Oh, not to-day," said Clarice blushing; "the weather is so fine that I have set my heart on a regular gipsying, and I mean to stay out till evening."

"Well, my dear, you know I never interfere with a holiday, and my cold is so bad I shall lie down in my own room. But when it gets a little cooler you might step down into the village and call at the vicarage, and leave those tracts I've covered for Mr Linton, and ask if he has any more ready."

Clarice nodded her head, but answered nothing. She, in fact, hardly knew what Miss Simmonds said, for she was studying the dinner, with a view to the viands that it might be possible to carry out to Olga. Soup? That, of course, was out of the question. Fish-balls? Yes! if she could manage to secure one. She had placed a large, clean handkerchief on her lap, and now, while the butler's back was turned, and Miss Simmonds' eyes were riveted on the table-cloth, she very skilfully contrived to manipulate a fish-ball from her plate to this handkerchief, the corners of which she threw over it. Then she could not restrain a little laugh at her own success.

"Did you speak, my dear?" said the governess.

"No, ma'am—no," she replied.

Roast chickens at Miss Simmonds' end of the table, cold sirloin of beef at her's. What extraordinary good luck! She certainly could carry off with her as much beef as she liked.

"Of course, I may give you chicken, Clarice?" said Miss Simmonds complacently. "I know you never eat cold meat when you can get hot."

"Oh! but on such a warm day as this my taste is capricious, and I'm going to eat beef for a variety."

She helped herself so largely as she spoke that she made the butler stare; and then, whenever an opportunity occurred, slipped a little slice into her handkerchief.

She believed she remained undetected, though at one time she saw Wilson's eyes fixed so earnestly on her that she felt herself colour violently; and then she could not help laughing as she thought how mystified he must be if he had really seen what she was doing.

Cherry pie and apricot jam tartlets. Again Clarice inwardly commented on her great good luck, for, of course, nothing could be so easy as to carry a tartlet away with her.

"I shan't eat any second course, my dear!" said Miss Simmonds.

"Then I'll take mine into the garden;—say grace, please"; and leaning her head forward, she thus flurried Miss Simmonds into at once saying grace, then hastily left the table, and hiding her little bundle in the flounced polonaise of her dress, and carrying the tartlets in her hand, she quitted the room while Wilson was still turned towards the sideboard, preparing the finger-glasses, and Miss Simmonds had not yet recovered from having been made to say grace before the proper time.

"I am in for a lecture on unladylike manners

when next I see my governess," was her impatient thought as she ran down the garden-walk. "Oh how tired I am of being under control! What could Olga mean by wishing there were only girls and boys in the world, and I desire so earnestly to be grown-up."

Olga was enchanted at the pic-nic meal which Clarice triumphantly laid before her. She took the provisions in her delicate little white hands, and declared it was most refreshing to eat without knives and forks.

"I wonder who the stupid fellow was who invented knives and forks *after* fingers had been made," said she. "Now, if the knives and forks had come first, it would have been clever enough, but they *were* so unnecessary with fingers."

When she had finished her dinner, she told Clarice that she had been thinking very seriously of her future plans, and that if nothing turned up soon, she thought she should go towards India.

"To India!" cried Clarice.

"No, not to India, because Papa and Mama are coming home, but *towards* India; and then I should probably meet them on the way."

"It is too great a risk," Clarice said. "Suppose you should miss them?"

"There's a risk in everything," replied she; "but

it's almost always easier to meet people than to miss them. Just think of all the people one is always meeting; that, I think, makes the risk so very little, that it is hardly any risk at all."

"But you don't know when you miss people," urged Clarice, after a moment's thought.

"Oh, don't I though?" cried Olga, "indeed, but I do. I miss Papa and Mama in one way and Mrs Jennings in another, and I know it quite well."

"Is she laughing, or is she a little deficient?" thought Clarice; and it was a thought that had more than once crossed her mind while talking with Olga.

"I don't know how we shall manage to-morrow," said she after a pause, "for I shall have my lessons to do; and I'm afraid you will be very lonely and dull."

"Let me have a lamp and some books in your favourite cupboard," said Olga, "and I shall do very well; and if I had writing things I might write a letter to Mama, perhaps, to explain to her what I've done; but they'll none of them like it. How odd it is that there is no law against grown-up people managing children! By what right are children ordered about, and always made to do what others tell them? They are just as free really, and *ought* to be just as free, as men and women. Animals only keep their young till they can feed themselves; and as soon as we can feed ourselves we ought to be turned loose. Don't you think so, Clarice?"

"I *was* thinking just now that I wished I was grown-up that I might not be under control; but it certainly never occurred to me to throw off the control beforehand."

"And yet, if all the children in the world determined to be free, how could it be prevented? There are a *great* many more children, you know, than grown-up people, so that we could quite easily get the upper hand."

And then Olga clapped her hands and laughed, and cried out how nice it would be, and what a pity it was all the children, all over the world, did not join together to emancipate themselves and each other.

"Mrs Jennings, my schoolmistress, is such a horrid old woman," said she;—"in the first place, she is quite horribly old, and then she is *very* foolish, and she is cross, and *all* her plans and rules are *always* bad. Now, there are just her, and three teachers, and five grown-up servants, and all the rest are girls—nearly forty girls and only seven or eight women! Now, is not it *silly* of the girls to *let* themselves be managed, instead of managing the handful of old people in the house."

"Boys do have barrings-out sometimes," said Clarice, thinking of Archer.

"Oh yes, *boys*!" cried the other disdainfully; "but then boys are so *much* better than girls, and boys do become their own masters very often while they are still boys—hardly older, you know, than you and I are. It's girls that are kept under and kept down; and so there's nothing left for girls but to run away, just as I did; and it would be hard to blame a poor creature for that."

"I shall be very sorry whenever you go from this, Olga," said Clarice. "I never had a girl companion before, and I'm getting so fond of you."

"Oh you dear!" cried Olga, kissing her. "Suppose I never go away, but that we always live together, like those two old creatures in North Wales. We must have an ornamented cottage, and lots of carved wood and scarlet geraniums, and wear men's hats."

Clarice laughed, and Olga laughed too, and said, "Oh Clarice, let us dance! it *is* such waste of time never to dance at all, all day," and she clasped Clarice in her arms, and waltzed her round and round for some minutes. But Clarice was very soon obliged to look at her watch, and to say now was the safe time for going home. They had been a little too late the night before, for the gardener, it turned out, had finished his tea, and come back to water his flowers; but this was just the time that they really might venture to steal through the garden, with no chance at all of being detected; "only if we are, you must not sing, Clarice," stipulated Olga—"we must never do the same thing two days running, if we can possibly help it, because that would be dull."

Clarice promised she would not sing; but then what should she do instead to warn Olga of danger?

"Yes, yes, you must sing! only you must sing all the way you go, and stop singing if anybody comes; and then when you stop I shall know that I am to hide more than ever—for I *am* hiding all the way, you know—and that will be just the reverse of what we did yesterday."

So the two girls returned to the house, Clarice singing as she went:

Must I search for everything?
  Will nothing do without me?
Is the glory of the spring
  Because I look about me?
Do the stars peep forth at night
  In answer to my searches?
Did I cause the silver light
  That glitters through the birches?

Chapter IV

Clarice and her father were not quite as chatty this evening as they had been the night before. Her mind was pre-occupied, and she could think of nothing but Olga. She had left her now in the dark closet with a candle, as she did not dare look for a lantern for her till the servants had gone to bed; and Olga had insisted on having the key, and locking herself in—making repeated promises that she would do nothing imprudent, and would take the greatest possible care that Ann should not suspect anything. Clarice was very uneasy as to how they should manage the next day. The whole morning, from breakfast-time till one o'clock, she would be obliged to spend in the library with Miss Simmonds. "If only," as she kindly thought, "her cold is so bad, that she gives me another holiday!" These bright summer holidays, passed with Olga in the glade, were delicious. Clarice was but little accustomed to the society of girls of her own age. She had some London cousins, who occasionally stayed with her or she with them, and whom she loved as well-disposed girls do love the relations they have known all their lives, but who are by no means particularly congenial to them; and she had a few young friends who lived in the neighbourhood; but Olga! she had never seen or talked with anybody in her life like Olga, who, with her quaint, un-English ways, her beauty, her caresses, and her conversation—sometimes so absurdly childish, sometimes so surprisingly clever, and always half-humorous, and illustrated by such enchanting bursts of laughter—had taken her heart by storm. Olga had told her that, as a child, she had had what she called a "lucky long fever"—lucky, because afterwards she was spoiled by every one, and in all things allowed to have her own way—a delightful doctor, who she was sure had been bribed by her smiles and kisses, having authoritatively pronounced that she was not to be thwarted, and that crying was particularly bad for her. "And so," cried Olga, "they all got into good habits, which they have kept up ever since, till that great mistake Papa made when he said, that when I was thirteen I was to go to school to be what is called *finished.*"

Clarice had said, with disdain, "Yes!" Olga replied, "And *finished* I should have been very soon, if, like a wise girl, as I am, I had not myself *finished* my school career still more quickly by running away."

Clarice sat now sipping her tea, and wondering how much of Olga's originality she inherited from her Danish mother, how much was entirely her own, and how much arose from the lonely, wild highland life she had led, and from her never having had intercourse with other children. What would Jane and Emily think of her? reflected she —her mind reverting to her London cousins—and she laughed softly to herself at the idea of bringing the quiet, well-trained town girls into contact with this strange lassie. They would think her either an idiot or wicked, and *I* think her both clever and good, she thought. Oh what a puzzle life is, and what a puzzle people are!—they and I agree very well; why am I sure we should feel so very very differently about Olga? How charming it would be if Papa would arrange with Olga's Grandmama that she should live with me, and be taught by Miss Simmonds! school-hours themselves would be

lively if Olga shared them; and she should sleep in the chintz room, and we could read and practise together, and talk for ever.

So far had Clarice's thoughts wandered on, and such was the charming future that her imagination had begun to sketch for her, when the door was suddenly burst open, and Ann—the staid, respectable Ann—dashed into the room, as white as a sheet of writing paper, and her cap half flying off her head.

"Mr Clavering!" cried she, "I've been and seen a ghost!"

Mr Clavering stared, and Clarice exclaimed. "Why did you do that Ann?" said he at length.

"Mr Clavering, I'm as innercent as the babe unborn. Miss Clarice, I beg your pardon if ever I said a cross word to you—I didn't ought to; and I'm afeared, Miss, I'm afeared the ghost is a bad sign for *you*."

"Ann!" said her master sternly, "I won't have you come here frightening your young lady, and putting nonsensical ideas into her head."

"No nonsensical ideas come from me, Mr Clavering—nor any ideas at all for that matter. I never had ideas, Sir, and nobody ever likened such a thing to me before, Sir. I've been respectable, and I've kep' respectable all my days, and I'm not standin' here to lose my character now—no, Sir, I'm not!"

"But the ghost, Ann?" cried Clarice, very much amused.

"I saw it in the little light there is now, Miss—a small white thing—all white—with white arms and legs, and a glory like round its head; and it whished by me on the stairs with the sound of a wind, and I never felt it though it touched me; and it turned upon me at the door of *your* room, Miss, and made awful signs at me with its white arms in the air; and it went in, and I was *that* frightened I followed it, but it had vanished, and there was nothin' to be seen, and nothin' to be heard but a little wailin' sound such as nothin' *could* make but a sperrit; so then I knowed what it was, and the real fear came on me, and I got down here somehow, and then Master set at me, and I'm all of a shake, Miss—I am indeed!"

"Well, Ann, I did not mean to hurt your feelings," said Mr Clavering penitently, "and I'm sorry you got such a start, but it's all nonsense, my good girl; you may take my word there's nothing in it, it was just some shadow or some light in the twilight; and I give you my word you shall never see this white thing again as long as you stay here."

"Well, Sir, I *was* thinking of making my stay short," said Ann, partly consoled; "I did come down to give warnin'."

"Warning? nonsense—if *you're* willing to lose a good situation for such stuff, *I'm* not going to part with a good servant. Wait a little—you'll see the ghost won't come back; the next time it makes its appearance you shall give warning if you like."

"Very well, Sir," said Ann doubtfully; "you've given me your word, but I don't much see what a gentleman's word can do against ghostses. Howsomever, I'll try to get over it this time; but it's the frightfulest thing as ever happened, and I feel as if I should never agin get a night's rest."

So saying, and curtseying respectfully, Ann left the room.

"My dear Clarice, you are quite pale!" said her father; "I do hope you are not so silly as to let what this girl says frighten you."

"No, Papa," replied Clarice, hardly above her breath.

"You don't know the curious effects of lights and shadows in a half-light," pursued he; "almost all the unexplained ghost stories in the world may be traced to that source; and the idea of a ghost in a modern house like this—half-a-mile from a railway-station, and only twenty miles from London itself—is preposterous."

"I don't think that is such a very good argument, Mr Clavering," said Miss Simmonds, who had followed Ann into the room, heard her story, and still stood near the door; "it is almost as if you believed ghosts *could* haunt old country-houses."

"Which I don't," said he, laughing; "and I'm sure Clarice is by far too sensible a girl to mind Ann's nonsense."

"If you feel the least uncomfortable, Clarice," said her governess, "I will sleep with you, or you may come into my room to-night."

Clarice's paleness was displaced by a bright blush at this good-natured proposition of her governess.

"Oh no, no! thank you," she cried hurriedly; "I am not the least afraid. I don't care a bit about sleeping by myself. I had *much* rather not."

"It was very kind of Miss Simmonds," said her father, with a hint of reproof in his grave voice, for he thought Clarice refused the offer a shade too vehemently; "but I agree with you, it is better not to accept her thoughtful proposal—it is better at once to put aside all idea of being made even a little uncomfortable for a single night by such utter nonsense. We should be too much at the mercy of the folly and ignorance of our fellow-creatures if we allowed such a thing as this to affect us."

"I am really not the least frightened, Papa," said Clarice, beginning to recover herself, and to be able to speak with composure, while she thought in her own mind, "Oh Olga, Olga! how I will scold you!"

When Clarice was released—for so uncomfortable and weary did Olga's sojourn in the house, and the necessity of concealing it from the others, make her, that she felt it quite as a release—when then she was released, and able to go up to her own room for the night, she went straight to the side of her bed, expecting to see a golden head on the pillow, but no golden head was there; then she sought the closet-door, and desired Olga to open it and come out. No answer. She pushed it, and it did not open. She called again to Olga, beseeching her not to be foolish, but to come out at once. A long, low, unearthly-sounding, wailing moan was the sole reply.

"If *that* was what you did at Ann, you foolish child, no wonder she was frightened. Come out, Olga; come out this minute!"

A lower, longer, more unearthly-sounding, more wailing moan, and that was all.

"Very well!" said Clarice, feeling some fear in spite of herself; "then I shall go away and call Papa, and tell him all about it. I can't bear this sort of thing any longer. You are making my life miserable, and it will be far better to tell Papa at once and have done with it."

Then the door flew open, and Olga came careering out. She had dressed herself in Clarice's handsome blue cloth riding-habit, which she allowed to trail behind her in a long train, and on her head she wore her high beaver hat. She had her silver-mounted whip in her hand, and she went cantering round and round the room with the habit rushing after her, slashing the whip in the air, and singing loudly and sweetly:

> If I had a donkey that wouldn't go,
> D'ye think I'd wollop him? Oh, no, no!
> I'd give him some oats, and I'd say "Gee woa!
> Come up! Neddy!"

We put all those notes of admiration to show the extreme spirit and expression with which Olga chanted the verse.

"Hush, hush! Olga, Olga! be quiet, pray, pray be quiet, you will be overheard, you will ruin everything!" cried Clarice, perfectly distracted.

But Olga did not stop till tired nature could no more, and breathless and exhausted she sank down on the floor, and lay there, looking like nothing in the world but yards of blue cloth wound about a black beaver hat. Clarice picked her up and pulled off the riding-gear, and there stood the little maiden in her white petticoat, with her lily-white neck and arms uncovered, and she lifted the latter up high in the air, and made strange cabalistic signs and weird faces at Clarice.

"Oh, naughty, naughty Olga!" said Clarice, laughing and kissing her, "that's how you played the ghost and frightened Ann."

"Yes," said Olga, "it was very nice—now I'm a ghost, but when you came in I was a policeman."

"A policeman!"

"Yes—didn't you guess?—well, I should have thought anybody would have guessed I was a policeman. Do you know, Clarice, I'm afraid you're rather stupid."

"But you'd nothing about you the least like a policeman."

"Oh, yes, *indeed* I had! you *might* have guessed."

"What nonsense, Olga, as if a policeman ever looked the least like *that*!"

"Ah, well, you've never been in Denmark; so how should you know?"

"You are very foolish, Olga," replied Clarice, decidedly nettled; "and I must assure you that there was nothing about you the least like a policeman."

"How unkind you are!" said Olga. "I think I'll go away."

"No, I'm not unkind—it's childish to say I'm unkind because I tell you the truth."

"And it's extremely unkind of you to say I was not like a policeman," replied Olga, pettishly; "however, it does not make a bit of difference, because I *know* I was."

"And *I* know you were not," cried Clarice, angrily. "In what way were you? what was there about you like a policeman?"

"Everything!" cried Olga. "There, you've asked me the question and I've answered it, so now you're bound to admit that I was—you've put it to the test yourself, so you must abide by *that*!"

"I've done nothing of the sort," replied Clarice coldly.

"Oh, that's not fair," said Olga; "if you're going to be unfair I've done with you; I hate that sort of thing; it's like the girls at school."

Clarice walked up and down the room greatly discomposed. "Olga," said she at last, "if you behaved in this sort of way at school I don't wonder that you were not happy there, or that the girls did not like you."

"I'm sure *I* never wondered a bit," replied Olga. "Nasty things!"

"And you had no right to put on my habit and hat without asking me."

"Yes, Clarice, *that* I had—because I wanted to be a policeman."

"Which you were *not*—nor the least like one; and you ought not to have gone about the house in your petticoat."

"Oh yes, Clarice, because *then* I was a ghost."

"Olga, you would wear out anybody's patience."

"And so would you, Clarice. I don't think I'll put up with it any more."

"Nobody in the world would suppose, from the way in which you talk, that you came here of your own accord, and that I am hiding you because you wish it. You seem almost to threaten me."

"I'm sure I don't wish to threaten you, Clarice," replied Olga, pouting, "and I never did the least before, and I wouldn't now, only you said I wasn't like a policeman."

"Because you were not. But you don't seem to understand—is it you who are hiding me, or is it I who am hiding you?"

"What's the use of going into extremes, Clarice, one way or the other? It's never a good plan—why shouldn't it be something between the two?"

"If you talk nonsense, Olga, I've done; I am quite serious and I thought you were also."

"So I was, but you won't let me, and then you scold me for not being what you won't let me be. I was a serious ghost, and I was a serious policeman, but you've sat upon me, and now it's all over!"

Olga put her two little hands together, and pouted out her rosy lips kissingly like a penitent saucy child, so saucy that even in its penitence its pretty impudence cannot be lost; and then a pitiful look came into her face, and she said, "I thought you loved me, Clarice!" and pouted out her lips again for a kiss.

"Oh, Olga, I do love you, but you must be good!" said Clarice, and took her in her arms, and gave the kiss so sweetly demanded, which the little creature returned twenty times, saying as she did so, "So I am, so I am, Clarice, I am good just now, just this minute—quick, quick, quick, Clarice! make me do whatever you want for it won't last—quick, Clarice, quick! Oh, Clarice, how slow you are—there's no hope now, for I'm not good any more—that minute's over!"

Then she ran up to the table where Clarice had put down what provisions she had been able to purloin for her supper, and ate and drank heartily, nodding her head before every sup of milk she took, and saying, "Your health, Clarice!"

After this the two girls went to bed. Clarice had twenty minds as to what she should do about locking her door. She knew it was wrong to disobey her father, and he had expressly desired her not to lock it—but then she could not trust to either Olga or herself waking in the morning before Ann called them, and if Ann discovered Olga in bed, what would become of the child? If her father had known about her he would surely not have desired her not to lock the door, so she locked it, determining that whenever he heard the history

(for it always seemed to Clarice that after Olga was safely restored to her Grandmother she should be at liberty to tell her father), she would confess to him how she had locked her door contrary to his orders. But Clarice's conscience was not satisfied, and finding how the concealment was leading her into errors, the idea for the first time crossed her mind whether the concealment itself might not be wrong.

Certainly the locking the door was a necessary precaution, for the sound sleep of youth which has scarcely ceased to be childhood, held the girls in its calm happy bonds, till Ann's hearty knocks at the door woke them in spite of themselves. Then again Clarice had to hustle Olga out of bed and into the cupboard before she admitted Ann.

"So you locked your door, Miss, again!" said that female grimly.

"Oh, Ann, you frightened me with your ghosts, you know," began Clarice; then she stopped, and a sudden rush of shame and horror came over her—she had *not* been frightened, that was *not* her reason—she was telling a falsehood!

"No, no, Ann!" she cried hurriedly, "that was *not* the reason, but please don't say anything about it—only that was *not* the reason, remember."

"Lawk, Miss," said Ann, "why should you be ashamed of being afeared of them ghosts? I'm sure nothin' in nature's more natural than to be afeared of strange creatures like they."

And she threw open the shutters and prepared her young lady's toilette for her.

After she was gone Olga was released, and the girls dressed themselves; but Clarice felt uncomfortable, and dissatisfied with herself.

It was very pleasant hiding Olga, but was it

right? This question haunted her, though she could not at present find any answer for it.

"You talk of something turning up, Olga!" she said abruptly; "what is it you expect to happen?"

"Oh!" cried Olga, in her careless way, "things are always either turning up or running down—that's all."

"But what is it you expect?"

"I don't expect anything much, dear," said Olga. "Did you never write a copy about not expecting much? Let me see—what is it? 'Expect little and reap mickle,' and 'Don't clutch or expect much.' I'm sure you've had to write those copies—now, havn't you, Clarice?"

"Nonsense, Olga! You know I havn't; but I wish you would answer seriously, for I am quite serious myself, and want to know."

"I wish you wouldn't be serious, Clarice—it's nasty."

"No, indeed, Olga! it's not nasty to be serious—not always nasty. I do want very much indeed to understand what it is you expect will happen."

"Oh!" cried Olga impatiently, "anything may happen. Mrs Jennings may trace me, or Grand-mama may inquire for me, or I may go towards India, or Papa and Mama may come home and find me, or I may run away from this some fine day if you tease me, Clarice, and get a nice girl to hide me."

"Yes, Olga, any of these things may happen, or none of them."

"Something will turn up—that you may be quite certain of. Did you ever know it all go on without something turning up? It couldn't, Clarice—that's my belief. It couldn't go on without something turning up."

"But why not?"

"Oh! because it never did."

"But what do you mean by *it*?"

"Oh, Clarice, what a question!"

"Yes! but what *do* you mean?"

"Why, of course, I mean what I say. What else *should* I mean?"

"But what do you mean by *it*?"

"Why, It, to be sure. No, no; you won't catch me that way. I know very well what I'm talking about."

"I declare, I don't believe you ever know what you're talking about, or ever mean anything."

"Clarice, shall we be able to spend to-day in the glade?"

"Ah! I much fear not. Certainly not till after dinner. Then, when I have to prepare my lessons for to-morrow, I might take the books out there,

6-2

as I sometimes do; and if Miss Simmonds is shut up safe with her cold, you might come too."

"What a blessed cold it is! Is it very heavy in her head, Clarice?"

"Yes, very heavy."

"Does she sniffle much?"

"Yes, you naughty child! she sniffles very much indeed."

"That's right. I think governesses ought always to have heavy colds in their heads, and sniffle a great deal;—it keeps them under."

Olga was obliged to consent to return to her den, while Clarice went to breakfast, after which Clarice brought her food as usual, and then left her with story-books and a candle. Olga kept the key, because she said she could not bear the feeling of being locked in, which Clarice willingly admitted *must* be very disagreeable. But she vowed that she would do nothing rash to-day, and would not get either herself or Clarice into any scrapes.

Chapter V

Clarice and Miss Simmonds sat together at their studies. It was past twelve o'clock, so the lessons has lasted for some hours, and they had been weary hours for both pupil and teacher. Clarice —clever, eager, and interested—generally liked her school-time well enough herself, and made it agreeable enough to her instructress. But what can be more wretched, than to learn without caring for, or attending to what you learn, except, indeed, attempting to teach one who is careless and inattentive!

Many times that morning had the patient governess, with a heavy cold in her head, and sniffling a good deal, asked Clarice what was the matter, and requested her to pay more attention, when Clarice would start, colour, beg pardon, and for a few minutes really occupy her mind with her lesson.

They were reading Tasso together, generally one of her favourite books, but even Rinaldo failed now to excite any interest, and she was languidly making utter nonsense of Italian phrases which Miss Simmonds knew she perfectly understood. They were seated on a sofa, at a little table at the opposite end of the room from the door, and facing it, when, without the slightest noise, the door suddenly opened, and Olga walked in. She advanced in total silence, and while they looked at her in amazement the silence in the room was intense, and yet her movements did not produce the least sound. She seemed to glide, not to walk, and Clarice could have declared her bare feet did not actually touch the ground—for her feet and legs were bare, so were her arms and neck, and their whiteness were really extraordinary. She was, in fact, all white, for she wore only her little short petticoat and bodice; and her face also looked, not pale, but very white. Then her bright, short crisp golden hair was all brushed up and about her head, standing out from it stiff and

burnished, like a halo. She advanced very quickly in that strange gliding way—paused for a moment opposite to them, with her eyes gazing vaguely forward—lifted her small slender white arms into the air, and in a weird manner, made strange cabalistic signs—then, without turning round, retreated as rapidly as she advanced, and passed through the door, which closed noiselessly after her. It was all the work of a moment, and Clarice, with a great feeling of fear which she hardly understood, looked breathlessly into her governess's face. It was ghastly pale, and her eyes stared as if they were dreaming and had not yet realised what they had seen.

"What was it—what was it?" she said at last, in an odd, frightened voice.

Clarice, not knowing what to say or do, remained silent.

"It was just what Ann said," Miss Simmonds cried; "it was just the same"; and then she began to tremble violently. "Clarice, did you see anything?"

"Oh, Miss Simmonds, it was nothing—indeed it was of no consequence—pray, don't think any more about it!"

Her governess looked at her, and with an immense effort, which did the conscientious woman, who considered her first duty was to her pupil, the greatest credit, recovered her self-possession. She put her hand to her forehead, and gave a faint, sickly smile. "My dear!" she said, "I have a bad cold, and I think I am not at all well. I will go into my own room and lie down. I am perhaps a little feverish. If I'm not better by-and-by I will send for Dr Smith."

With a great pang of remorse, Clarice took her hand and kissed it. "I really don't think there is anything wrong, dear, dear Miss Simmonds!" she said; "but do go and rest yourself—it will be much better; and please don't mind—you are frightened, but there is nothing to be frightened at; I am quite sure there is not."

"No, no, dear!" said the other, and kissed her forehead. "I will go and keep quiet, and give you a holiday for the rest of the day. I did not mean to have dinner at any rate, for my head is so heavy with my cold, and I ordered myself some broth in my own room—so you won't see me again for some time."

She spoke more cheerfully, and Clarice felt relieved; she was too young and ignorant to clearly understand what Miss Simmonds' fears were, and she hoped they had passed away, and would disturb her no more; and in the reaction of feeling she could hardly help laughing when she thought of the naughty, clever child, who had acted a ghost so well. Still, when Miss Simmonds had left her, she did not join Olga at once, but walked up and down the library in uneasy meditation.

Could this concealment be right that led to so much that was undoubtedly wrong? True; if you hid the King you might have to tell a falsehood to save his life, but then you would tell that falsehood to a traitor. It was not a traitor that she *had* disobeyed when she locked her door at night, or had began to tell an untruth to when she opened it in the morning, or whom now she had allowed to be deceived and frightened; it was her own familiar friends, the members of her own household, her father, her servant, and her governess. Could this be right? But then, how could she help it? Could it have been right to refuse help to a fellow-creature in distress? Still more, could it, by any possibility, be right to betray that fellow-creature when she had promised to assist her? Poor Clarice! so false was the position in which she had placed herself, that her duties seemed to conflict, and whatever she did must be wrong. She was not in the least a girl to shilly-shally if once she saw clearly the path of duty. If she perceived she had left it, she would bravely confess her fault and retrace her steps; but with the thoughtless presumption of youth, and, perhaps, more especially, of her own individual character, she had done a thing without an instant doubting that it was a right thing to do, and only now was she beginning to think that perhaps she was mistaken, and that her act had been wrong.

After a good deal of uncomfortable thought, during which she found herself quite unable to come to any conclusion, she went up-stairs, but she did not find Olga there. Oh, well! she said impatiently, of course she is in the glade; and so towards the glade she turned her steps; but though she searched all through it, looking under every bush and up into every tree, she saw nothing of Olga. Then she felt a conviction that Olga was gone; the volatile, capricious creature, had tired of life here, and, as she had herself threatened, had gone somewhere else, to find a nice girl to hide her.

"Of course I am glad!—of course I am very glad!" Clarice repeated over and over again to herself; but, even as she said the words, a feeling of profound depression came over her, and her heart within her felt as if it was made of lead.

After a while she returned to the house and ate her solitary dinner; then, with the inconsistency of love, though convinced Olga had left her, she hid provisions for her in a drawer in her bedroom, and stood for a minute or two sorrowfully regarding the little hoard which her reason told her she had hidden in vain.

What should she do with herself, through all the long, lonely, melancholy hours of this summer afternoon and evening? Her eye fell on the parcel of books Miss Simmonds had asked her to take to the Parsonage the day before. Ah, how thoughtless she had been! how she had forgotten everything but Olga while Olga was with her. Now she could remember her duties, for Olga was gone! She should be glad of the walk; it would be something to do, and she was in no mood for that idleness which is so sweet a thing to the happy—so intolerable to those whose hearts are ill at ease; so she took the books rejoicing that the errand had offered itself, and in the full blaze of summer splendour above and about, but not within her, went out. Half-a-mile brought her to the village in which stood the church and pretty, rural-looking parsonage. Once, as she went, her imagination played her a trick, and she thought for an instant she heard Olga's chuckling laugh of irrepressible glee; but, even as she looked about her, she knew it was not so, and she saw nothing but a linnet in the tree above her head, which sang out, almost angrily, a few loud notes, and flew away.

Mr Linton was at home, and Clarice, whom he had known all her life, was shown into his study.

"Do you want my wife?" said he, "or shall I do? She has got her singing class in the laundry, but could spare you five minutes."

"Oh no! you will do; in fact, my message is to you. Miss Simmonds has sent back those books we have covered, and is ready for more."

"And more are ready for her. I am very much obliged to her. She is an invaluable person, Clarice. I sometimes wonder whether you appreciate her."

"I'm sure I don't know," replied Clarice, sighing wearily.

"You will when you are grown up; but perhaps you do now; only great helps are often not recognised till we have lost them. It is when you miss a thing that you can classify it, and learn what it really is worth."

"Yet sometimes we could 'better spare better men,'" said Clarice, thinking of Olga.

Mr Linton, who had been sorting out the little books from a heap on the table, looked up and laughed. At that moment the servant entered the room, and laid a card down before him.

"A lady, Sir, who wants to see you on particular business!"

"Mrs Jennings!" said he, glancing at the card; "now, who can she be?"

Clarice's heart stood still for a moment, then gave a great bound, and went on beating with a rapidity that frightened her.

"Mrs Jennings!" Then it was all over. Olga had been traced. The schoolmistress had come on purpose to find her, and everything would be discovered. How unfortunate that she was here! What a pity that she could not get away! But, even while these thoughts chased themselves wildly through her mind, Mrs Jennings was ushered into the study. A very small woman, in a long grey cloak, with a straw bonnet and thick veil, which she kept down. Not a very awful outside, at any rate, thought Clarice.

"Mr Linton, I believe," said the schoolmistress in a cracked voice.

"Can I be of any use to you?" was the civil reply.

"I came to make inquiries, Sir, into Mr Clavering's character!"

"Into Mr Clavering's character?" repeated the astonished clergyman.

"Yes, Sir, into Mr Clavering's character."

"Mr Clavering, Ma'am, is my friend. But I really cannot feel justified in answering any questions about him. Let me introduce you to his daughter, Miss Clavering."

The little woman bent her head stiffly towards Clarice, and Clarice, feeling a good deal affronted, returned the salute with equal stiffness.

"I have reason to believe, Sir, that Miss Clavering is shortly to be sent to school, and I wished to put in a word for my Seminary for Young Ladies."

"Really, Ma'am, I must refer you to Mr Clavering himself—I have nothing whatever to do with his affairs."

"What does she mean, Mr Linton?" cried Clarice. "Is Papa thinking of sending me to school?"

"I have not heard a whisper like it, I assure you—I really think the lady is under some mistake."

Then he glanced down at the card; "'Mrs Jennings, Clevelands'—why that is in Yorkshire. I beg your pardon, Ma'am, there is some great misunderstanding. You are not Mrs Jennings of Clevelands; I have the pleasure of being acquainted with that lady."

A pause; and the little grey figure shook either

with fear or with suppressed laughter, and then replied; "I never said I was Mrs Jennings, Sir."

"Excuse me, Ma'am; you sent in her card."

"Yes, because it was the only one I had about me," was the reply.

"An odd reason, surely. You will excuse me, Ma'am, but I am a busy man; and perhaps I may consider that your business with me is over."

"Certainly, Sir," said the little woman, rising—"and as for Miss Clavering, I hope that she and I shall become better acquainted when her Papa entrusts her to my care."

She turned her back on Mr Linton and faced Clarice—lifted up her veil, showed the features of Olga, which were the next moment distorted into a hideous grimace—put her veil down, dropped a stiff curtsey, and saying, "Bless you—bless you both," in a very cracked voice, walked out of the room.

"Mad, I think!" said Mr Linton; but at the same time he rang the bell, and desired the maid to have an eye after the hats and umbrellas in the hall, and to be sure that the lady left the house without visiting any of the other apartments. These orders gave Clarice a few seconds to recover from the state of bewilderment into which she had been thrown; and as she recovered, the excitement of her feelings vented itself in irrepressible laughter. She was immensely diverted at Olga's bit of acting, and she sat and laughed till she could laugh no longer. Mr Linton caught the infection and laughed heartily too.

"And do you actually know Mrs Jennings?" asked she at last.

"Yes; a very respectable lady who keeps a school in Yorkshire; but a tall, gaunt, raw-boned woman who would make twenty of that little hop-o'-my-thumb."

"Is it a good school?"

"You are not really thinking of what she said?—imagining that your father has any idea of sending you there? If he had—but I am certain it is mere nonsense—I should assuredly recommend him *not.* It may be called a good school, and it is undoubtedly a fashionable school, but in my opinion Mrs Jennings is not a judicious woman, and I should not advise any parents to send their daughters to her."

"Well, I must be going, I think," said Clarice, getting up and putting her hand out for the books.

"Wait a few minutes, my dear, and I will walk home with you. I really think that little lady is mad, and if you came across her on the road it might not be pleasant for you to be alone."

"Oh, no, please don't, I am not a bit afraid," said Clarice.

> Oh, what a tangled web we weave,
> When first we practise to deceive,

thought she, with a great sigh. Here she was now forced to act a part towards Mr Linton as she had before had to do to her father, to Miss Simmonds, and to Ann. "One thing is certain," said she to herself, "whatever it may be right for me to do, now that I am in for it, and have taken upon myself a duty towards Olga, I will never practise a concealment again—I will never put myself into such a position as this again—I was free to take the first step or not to take it, and all that has followed is the consequence of that step. Such a step as that, voluntarily to enter into a concealment, which must be kept up towards those to whom I owe a duty, I will never take again. I feel almost sure that I must have been wrong when I consented to hide Olga; how strange it is that it never occurred to me at the moment that I was doing wrong!" Mr Linton walked home with her, and she was in an agony of fear all the way. Without an atom of confidence in Olga's discretion, each moment she was expecting her to appear. She knew that she was capable of leaping down on them from the top of a tree, springing up at them from the bottom of a ditch, and masquerading in any character besides her own. It is like having a wild animal to deal

with, thought poor Clarice, or one of those spirits that are half-good and half-evil, but are always off their balance, so that you cannot reckon on them for two minutes together. Two minutes? I would not reckon on Olga for half-a-minute, or for half half-a-minute. Lost in these reflections—now glancing anxiously round her, now shutting her eyes for fear she should see what she was looking for—Clarice did not appear to Mr Linton to be as intelligent a companion as usual; and when, after a long speech he had made, which ended with the words, "Do *you* think so, Clarice?" she replied, "Oh, yes, by all means"; he said very quietly, "I don't believe you have heard a single word I said to you." She could only give a little nervous laugh, beg his pardon, and confess that she had been thinking of something else.

"I believe that gray woman frightened you, and that you are really afraid your father means to send you to school."

Clarice blushed, but protested that she was not at all afraid of that; she had too often heard Mr Clavering express his dislike to schools to have any doubt on that head.

They reached the house just after Mr Clavering's return from London. He was delighted to see Mr Linton, and insisted on his staying to dine with him. The two men were old friends, and, though widely different in character and pursuits, valued each other truly, and sincerely enjoyed each other's society. When she had seen the dining-room door close upon them, Clarice went to pay Miss Simmonds a visit. She was lying down, had slept, and pronounced herself to be a great deal better, though she had still a nervous look about her, and said she thought she would keep quite quiet for the rest of the day. Clarice left the books with her, told her Mr Linton had accompanied her home, and was dining with her father, and then went to her own room, which she entered with a beating heart. But neither in the room nor in the closet did she find Olga.

"This worry is intolerable," she said aloud. "The whole thing must be put a stop to; one can't go on in this way for the rest of one's life, which is what it seems coming to."

Happy Clarice! who was still so young that two days seemed to her as a large portion of her life—strange that when the days stretch far before us such is the case, and when they are few each day seems to us like only an hour.

While she was leisurely dressing herself for the evening, and wondering what would be the next step in the curious drama wherein she found herself acting a prominent part, she was interrupted by Miss Simmonds coming into her room without knocking at the door, and in a hurried, agitated manner.

"My dear Clarice!" she said, "I am not so well, and I wish to send for Doctor Smith. I don't like disturbing your father, who is at dinner with Mr Linton. Do you think William could run down to the village for the doctor? You see the evening is closing in, and if I wait much longer it may be too late for him to come."

"Oh yes, certainly. I am sure you may give your own orders, dear Miss Simmonds—but I am so sorry you are worse—what is it?—you seemed better I thought—what do you feel now?"

"Never mind, love—I fancy I must be a little feverish—what ails me is of no real consequence. I have read of the same thing occurring to others; but it is distressing, and I am sure I ought to see the doctor."

"Then will you send for him at once, or shall I?"

"I will—but I thought it would be best to mention it to you, because then you can tell Mr Clavering when you go down stairs to tea."

"But I hope you are not feeling ill?"

"No—no—don't fret yourself. I shall tell Doctor Smith what is the matter, and I have no doubt he will soon set me right again."

And so Miss Simmonds went away, and Clarice wondered what it meant—she had never seen her governess look so pale, or heard her speak in such a hurried, nervous manner.

Soon afterwards Olga walked into the room quite self-possessed, and in a very leisurely way, as if the house belonged to her, and she was hiding from nobody. She looked steadily at Clarice, who looked steadily at her; then she made the same hideous grimace with which she had greeted Clarice at the parsonage, and then they both burst out laughing because they could not help it.

"Oh, wasn't it fun?" cried Olga at last.

"But so foolish, so daring, so reckless!" said Clarice. "How could you do it? You will get into some awful scrape, Olga—I am sure you will."

"Oh, wasn't it fun?" repeated Olga, swaying backwards and forwards with laughter as she spoke; "and to think of you not knowing me, and to think of *his* knowing Mrs Jennings! Oh, Clarice, Clarice, wasn't it fun?"

"Well, no doubt it was very amusing, but it was very wrong, Olga, and you ought not to have done it."

"Of course I ought not to have done it—one never ought to do fun—but it's delicious, Oh, it's delicious. Poor dear old thing! what did he say when I was gone?"

"He said you were mad, and he told the maid to have an eye after the hats and umbrellas."

"And how angry you were at my making enquiries about your father—and my saying he was going to send you to school. Oh—Oh—Oh—wasn't it fun? I declare I didn't know I was half such a genius—how well I did it! Oh, wasn't it fun?"

And Olga laughed, and Clarice laughed whether she would or no.

"How did you get there? did you know I was there?" said she at last.

"I went with you all the way, hiding and scuffling, and you never saw me. Once I thought you heard me laugh, you looked about so, but I was miles off in a minute, and then I watched you into the house, and then I followed you. Oh, Clarice, *wasn't* it fun?"

"Yes; but have you been fright'ning Miss Simmonds again? because I can't allow that, Olga—I can't, indeed. You mustn't do it."

"It was only just for a little minute—such a little minute," said Olga. "I was exploring, and I explored into her room, and she lay there with her eyes shut, and I stood at the foot of the sofa and made signs at her, and she opened her eyes and gave a loud scream, and I ran off and hid. Why should she be frightened at me? a silly! I might just as well be frightened at her; but I was such a little minute, Clarice, that it could not be very naughty—nobody could be *very* naughty in such a nice little minute as that."

Chapter VI

When Clarice went down stairs, she found that Dr Smith, having paid Miss Simmonds a visit, was sitting talking with her father and Mr Linton in the drawing-room. It was dusk, and they continued their conversation without perceiving her.

"It is a curious case," Dr Smith was saying. "She thinks she has twice seen the figure your servant describes as a ghost—of course she is far too sensible a woman to believe in ghosts, and therefore she has no doubt she is ill, and requires medical aid. I can detect no signs of illness except a common cold, but she has acted wisely, and I have prescribed for her, and hope she will be all right in a day or two."

"I suppose it might be the beginning of an illness?" asked Mr Clavering.

"I hope not; for, as I said, there is no other sign of it—nothing in the pulse, or the skin, or the eye, to denote fever; I think it will just pass off, and we shall hear no more about it. Oh, Miss Clavering, I beg your pardon, I did not see you; how do you do?"

They shook hands, lights were rung for, and Clarice made the tea.

Mr Linton took up the newspaper. "I have been kept so busy all day," said he, "I have not even had a moment to look at the *Times*."

"That is only the advertisement half," replied Mr Clavering, "the other is in my office; I will send for it if you like."

"No, no, I've got hold of the agony column, at which I seldom look; now I'll take a peep into the mysteries that are going on in the world. Listen to this: 'Willie, return and all shall be forgiven; you shall have the best bed-room, and your aunt shall not be consulted'—what an uncommon fool Willie must be. Now, here's another: 'Ogre to Pual. Shut that Piano—Asparagus.' And here's a long one: '£10 Reward.—Absconded from a school in the North of England '—Mrs Jennings', perhaps, Clarice, that's in Yorkshire, you know—'with stolen money and jewels to the amount of more than £50, a girl of fifteen, a sort of upper servant and junior teacher, short and slight, with blue eyes, fair complexion, and light hair, dressed in a grey cloak, and straw bonnet with thick veil.' Hullo!" cried Mr Linton, interrupting himself, "why, that really *is* like her—'dressed in a grey cloak, and straw bonnet and thick veil,' and then, 'a girl of fifteen' and 'short and slight'—why, she was no bigger than a child; but then, what could make her come to me in that way? it's very odd, upon my word it's very odd," and he ran his fingers through his hair and looked round at the others in a sort of an appealing way, adding hastily. "Why, Clarice, I have quite startled you—are you ill?"

"It can't be her—Oh, I'm sure it can't be her," cried Clarice faintly, and then she leant back in her chair, shuddered painfully, and burst into tears, for a dreadful doubt had seized upon her. Surely it *must* be Olga, the description was so exact, and, if so, Olga had deceived her, she was a wicked impostor and a thief! She thought of the money and the jewels, and her heart sank within her, and she felt as if it must break.

"My dear child! there's nothing to be frightened or distressed about," said Mr Linton, "even if my visitor and this absconder *are* the same, and that is more than doubtful, only the resemblance in some points is curious. I'll tell you what, I'll certainly make some inquiries about her in the village and at the station; one may just as well find out what one can, but I don't think it will have to go into a court of justice, or that you need appear as a witness," he added, laughing.

Horror upon horror! Clarice seemed hardly able to breathe. "I am sure she is not a thief," she gasped out. The three gentlemen looked at her in surprise.

"Why should you care?" asked her father, to whom Mr Linton had related the afternoon's adventure at dinner-time.

"I had no notion you had taken a fancy to her," said the clergyman.

"Drink your tea, and don't think any more about such nonsense," said the Doctor.

At that moment there was a loud ring at the house bell, and Wilson brought in a message to Mr Clavering that a man wanted to see him. Mr Clavering, like many city men, disliked the smallest approach to activity after dinner. "Show him in here," he said, rather crossly, and a respectable-looking person was ushered into the drawing-room. Mr Clavering enquired his business, and the man told his story as follows:

The day before he had been passing down the lane that skirted Mr Clavering's grounds, and, in the little wood at the end of the garden, he saw a girl kneeling among the grass, and packing, as it seemed to him, a small travelling-bag. He thought this so odd that he stood still, out of curiosity, and watched her over the hedge, and he distinctly saw her picking up money and jewels from the ground and stuffing them into this bag; he saw gold, and bright, glittering things he believed to be diamonds. To-day he met the same girl on the road—on the former occasion he thought she looked like a lady, but now she had on a grey cloak and straw bonnet like a servant. She had her veil up when he met her, and he had no doubt it was the same girl. He felt so curious to see what she was about that he followed her at a distance, and he saw her stop at the Parsonage, ring the bell, and, after a time, go in. He concluded that she was some visitor either at Mr Clavering's or at the Parsonage, and should have thought no more about her if he had not happened to take up the newspaper at the public-house afterwards, and read an advertisement about a girl having run off with money and jewels. Here he produced the paper from his pocket, and showed Mr Clavering the advertisement that Mr Linton had just been reading aloud to them, and he said the description, both of the girl and her dress, exactly suited the young person he had seen in the wood. He was very much struck by this advertisement, and he took the liberty of going to the little wood, and searching about in the place where he had seen the girl packing the things up, and there he had actually found a five-pound note and a pearl ring. Then he went to the station, and, in reply to his enquiries, he learned that a girl answering to his description had arrived two days before by a northern train, and the school the servant had absconded from, he pointed out to Mr Clavering, was stated to be in the north, that she travelled third-class, and, though her ticket was for London, stopped at this station, twenty miles short of it, and got out. Altogether, he thought the circumstances so very suspicious that he had gone first to the Parsonage, where he heard that Mr Linton was dining here. He questioned the servant about the visitor in a grey cloak, and she told him, master had ordered her, in a great hurry, to have an eye to the hats and umbrellas when she left. So he had come on here, where he knew he should find Mr Clavering and Mr Linton together, and he thought the best plan was to tell them all about it, and they would advise him as to what he ought to do—of course what he wanted was to get the reward, and he thought he was on the high road to it, but was a little puzzled as to the next step. The gentlemen

heard him with a good deal of interest, especially Mr Linton, who kept ejaculating, when the girl's visit to him was alluded to, "How very odd!"

"I can't in any way account for that part of it," said he, "if she *is* the thief, except by supposing that she is out of her mind."

"At any rate, my man," said Mr Clavering, "there seems only one course for you to take—you must put it into the hands of the police—go to the police-sergeant, give up the property to him, and set him on the track. The thief will certainly not escape, and you will get a fair portion of the reward for your information—the whole of it, perhaps, as you will have already restored some of the property, and the rest will be recovered through your means—at any rate, you will get enough to make this line of conduct quite worth your while."

The man thanked him, and said he had no doubt that was the best thing he could do; and he was sure that if either of the gentlemen were called on to give evidence, or take any action in the matter, they would not forget that, but for him, nothing would have been known about this girl, and that he had at once given up the money and the ring, when he might have held his tongue about them, and kept what would certainly be worth more than even the whole of the ten pounds reward.

"You have behaved very well," said Mr Clavering; "and if it shall be necessary, we will bear witness in your favour."

"Honesty always is the best policy," added Mr Linton; "and we will take care that you find it so in this instance."

So, reiterating his thanks, the unexpected visitor took his leave.

White as a sheet, and more miserable than she had ever felt before in her whole life, sat Clarice, listening to every word that was said, and feeling that every word as it was spoken made Olga's innocence impossible.

Oh that she had never seen her! Oh that she had never listened to her! Oh that she had never concealed her in her father's house, without her father's knowledge! By the consequences of her conduct she saw her fault; but she was far too sensible and too good a girl not to be aware that the fault would have been just the same had the consequences been widely different.

To a feeling really of agony that Olga should be wicked, succeeded a wild desire to know what she ought now to do herself. Give her up to justice, to be tried, condemned, put in prison?—that was impossible. She felt anger, contempt, and dislike for the creature who had so shamefully deceived her; but she had loved her, kissed her, slept by her side, and thought her the most bewitching child that she had ever met. And she was *such* a child, and so clinging, so loving, so sweet; to think of her in a prison among common felons, made Clarice feel sick, and leaning back in her chair, she turned all the colours of the rainbow, got hot and cold, and thought the room was receding from her, and that there was nothing solid left in the world; in fact, she almost fainted.

"Miss Clavering," said Doctor Smith, "The heat of the weather has upset you as well as Miss Simmonds. Take my advice, and go to bed, and put thieves, and impostors, and girls in grey out of your head. Go up into your own room, read an amusing novel for half-an-hour, and then a sound sleep will scatter all your fears to the winds, and you will wake in the morning quite yourself."

"It is very unlike Clarice to be so easily upset," said her father kindly. "Good-night, my love; and let me see you with your own face to-morrow instead of that pale, frightened one that I hardly seem to recognise."

Mechanically she kissed her father, and shook hands with the others, then, taking her candle, walked up-stairs like a person in a dream. But she woke with a sudden shock when she came to the door of her room. What a scene was before her! She must accuse Olga of her guilt, hear her confession, endeavour to awake a feeling of repentance within her, and then send her away. To harbour her any longer was as impossible to Clarice as it was to give her up into the hands of justice. The only course that she considered open to her was to make her wander forth in the night, and seek for shelter elsewhere. There was a railway-station three miles distant, to which she could easily walk, and where no inquiries about her had been made.

But Clarice was determined on one thing. She should not take her stolen property with her. She should leave it behind, and when she was really gone, Clarice could at once seek her father, tell him everything, place the things in his hands, and patiently submit to his displeasure, and to any punishment he might award to her fault.

Olga must have friends, and to these she would insist on her going; and then, perhaps, in time her old tranquil life, that now seemed so far—so very far off, might come back to her, and she might some day almost forget that Olga had ever been here.

At last she took courage. By a desperate effort she opened the door, and, walking into the room, looked round her, like one who knows some horrible sight awaits her, which she must brave, but will not, because she must brave it, try to disguise from herself that it is horrible.

Olga lay on the bed, looking like a cherub, and sleeping like an infant.

Clarice put the candle down on the table, and went up to the side of the bed.

"Olga, get up!" she said, but she did not touch her; she shrank from the idea of ever touching her again.

Olga opened her blue eyes as a flower unseals its petals.

"Oh you dear Clarice!" she cried, "I am so glad you have come! I was so lonely that I went to sleep." And she pouted out her lips in the pretty childish way in which she invited kisses, but no kiss came from Clarice's lips to hers.

"You are discovered!" she said very sternly. "I know all about you—who you are, and what you have been doing. You are a wicked girl, and you must go away from this!"

"Oh no!" said Olga smiling; "I'm not really wicked. I make-believe much worse than I am; and I won't *think* of going away, dear Clarice!"

"Olga, don't talk in this way," replied Clarice almost violently; "I can't bear it. You must go away; and you must leave the money and jewels behind you. I can't let you take them with you."

"Why, then, Clarice, it's you that are wicked," said Olga, laughing; "only I know you're not,

because you're *particularly* good. But fancy you turning me out of doors, and keeping all my things! Why, you'd be a thief, Clarice!"

"Olga, *you* are a thief! and I know it. How dare you use the word when you are the thing itself?"

Olga opened her innocent blue eyes wide, and fixed them earnestly on Clarice.

"I am not a thief!" she said, with a little scorn in her sweet, young voice.

"Don't, Olga—don't! You are adding to your sins by each word you say. I know everything, and you can't deceive me. They have advertised for you!"

"My goodness!" cried Olga—"advertised for *me*!"

"There is a reward offered!"

Then Olga began to laugh. "What fun!" she said. "Oh, do tell me; what am I worth?—what's my price, Clarice?"

"Olga, you make me shudder!" said Clarice; "don't—pray don't. I know that you are a servant and a thief!—it is all in the paper. You can't deceive me. Pray confess everything at once, and let us have done with it."

"I a servant and a thief!" cried Olga. "Fancy a Leslie being a servant and a thief!"

"But you are not a Leslie—you are a servant! and you have told me nothing but falsehoods. What is your real name?"

"My name is Olga Leslie."

"Well, of course, it may be Olga Leslie, but it is very unlikely."

"And it is *extremely* unlikely that yours is Clarice Clavering!"

Clarice was silenced by this rejoinder.

"I don't know one bit what you mean, Clarice," continued Olga; "but, of course, you *don't* mean that I'm a thief, because that would be such nonsense. Ladies are never thieves, of course! What do you mean by a thief? Do you mean a person who steals?"

"Yes!" said Clarice quietly, "I mean a person that steals."

"But you don't mean that *I* have stolen anything?"

"Yes, I do! I mean that you have stolen that money and those jewels you keep in your bag, and have run away from school—in which you were a servant, and that there is an advertisement in the newspapers telling all about it!"

Olga's cheeks grew very pink, and her eyes glittered like pieces of turquoise blue sky on which the sun is shining; she sat up in a little curled heap on the bed, and, clasping her small white hands together, looked earnestly and steadfastly full into Clarice's face.

"It's not true!" she said, in a voice clear and bright as a bell—"it's a wicked advertisement, made by some bad old person. Oh Clarice, how *could* you believe it!"

Clarice returned the gaze as steadfastly as it was

given;—she looked down into Olga's eyes, and thought she saw her heart in them. A shiver of hope ran through her whole frame, and an unshakable faith sprang up to meet it. She sank down on her knees, clasped her arms round the little white creature on the bed, and let tears come freely, that would not be repressed. "Oh Olga!" she cried—"dear little Olga!—poor innocent little Olga! Oh forgive me—forgive me!"

Olga cried too, but she kissed the tears off Clarice's cheek, while she said, "How could you, Clarice? how could you believe anything horrid about poor little me? *I* couldn't believe anything against *you*—not if all the bishops came to me *in* their aprons and *swore* to it—because I know and I love you—so I *couldn't*; and to think I was a thief! Oh, Clarice! why, a thief is worse than anybody else. I'd rather be a murderer, for he's not so *mean*!"

"Forgive me, Olga—dear, dear Olga, forgive me!" was all Clarice could say.

"Oh, to be sure, I forgive you!" cried Olga briskly; "one never can help forgiving—can one? But what could make anybody say such things about me in an advertisement? What a bad old person it must be! and what do they say, dear? do they give my name?"

"No, they don't give your name"; and Clarice repeated the words of the advertisement as well as she could recollect them.

"But what a horrid shame!" said Olga. "Why, the money is what Grandmama sent me; and she gave me the jewels too—they belonged to her favourite daughter who died—and as Grandmama loves me ever so much better than she does Aunt Jessie, she gave me all her girl's things (for poor young Aunt Annie died when she was but a girl); so I didn't like leaving them behind me—and then to say I stole them!—how very *very* wicked grown-up people are, Clarice!"

"And there is a five-pound note and a pearl ring you left in the glade, and a man has found them and given them to the police."

"What! half my money, and my pretty pearl ring. Oh what a shame!—why then, the man is the real thief *and* the police! Oh Clarice, *do* you think *we* could get the reward by giving up that man and the police instead of me?"

Clarice was by this time able to laugh, which she did at this idea, and Olga, always ready for a laugh, joined her.

"Oh, Olga," she kept saying, "I am so sorry, but I am so glad—Oh, so very glad!"

"Yes!" said Olga, "It's just as well I'm not a thief for all parties; and what *can* make them say I'm a servant and a teacher? A Leslie a servant! and as to being a teacher—why, I'm sure I never taught anybody anything in my life, and for a very good reason too—I couldn't! Why I don't *know* anything well enough to teach it—it would be a wise school that hired me as teacher—wouldn't it, Clarice?"

"I do think, Olga, that we must do something now—it will be dreadful if you are found out here; they'll want to put you in prison, and you're not steady enough to hide. You're sure to be found out. I think the best plan will be for you to write to your Grandmama and tell her all about it, and then she'll let you know what you are to do; and she might write and tell Papa. It is of no use for *us* to tell him now, because they are all persuaded that the advertisement is true."

"But Grandmama is not at home."

"Yes, but if you direct it home, and put 'To be forwarded' on the direction, it will be sent to her."

"Well," said Olga, reluctantly, "I suppose I must; but Grandmama won't be at all pleased, and half the good of being here will be gone when I've told. It is so nice being somewhere when everybody thinks you're nowhere at all."

Chapter VII

Worn out with excitement, Clarice slept soundly that night, though she awoke to a day that she felt would be full of cares.

She had truly stated that Olga was not steady enough to hide, and this unsteadiness of Olga's was, next to the necessity of concealment which she had brought upon herself, her principal trouble.

It would now be so very dangerous for her to stir from the one room; and yet she felt convinced, that notwithstanding all she could say, and all Olga would promise, when the temptation to leave it came, she would not be strong enough to resist it. And if any one saw her now she would be lost. No grown-up person—certainly no grown-up man, Clarice felt sure, would believe in her innocence—and yet, on that innocence, Clarice would fearlessly have staked her life—therefore if she was found, she would be taken up, tried, put in jail, and considered as a thief. Clarice longed to pour out the whole history to her father, or to Mr Linton, but she felt too sure of what the result would be; they would be very sorry for her individually (though of course her father would be very angry with her too), would tell her that she was a foolish, good-natured child—had been sadly imposed upon—and that justice must be permitted to take its course. She hated that phrase which she had heard gentlemen use, that "Justice must take its course." She could just fancy the quaint things that Olga would say about it, and she considered it to mean that people were content to be unkind, while in her creed unkindness itself was unjust.

Miss Simmonds was better, but followed Doctor Smith's advice by keeping quiet in her own apartment, so after breakfast Clarice was able to join Olga in her bedroom, where it was supposed she would spend an hour or two in writing Italian exercise and doing German translation. The first duty, however, was to make Olga write her letter to her Grandmother, to which act that young lady was extremely averse.

"I don't think I will, Clarice," she said; "Grandmama *will* fumble her fingers so when she gets it. She always does when she's fidgeted; and I don't think I ought to make Grandmama fumble her fingers."

"Nonsense, Olga!"

"Well, Clarice, I oughtn't to do what I think I oughtn't."

"You *must* do this. You said you would last night. There's no help for it. It's the only thing left that can be done."

"No, it isn't!"

"Why, what else is there?"

"Oh! I might go towards India, or I might go to jail."

"Do be serious, Olga—just for half-an-hour, if you can—just till you have written this letter!"

"But I don't mean to write the letter. I think, after all, I'll go to jail!"

"There's a sheet of paper, and here are pen and ink. Now, begin."

"Do you know, Clarice, I don't think I shall dislike going to jail!—just for a little bit, you know. I was thinking it over last night, and there are several good points about it. I believe, on the whole, it will be rather nice."

"Where does your Grandmama live?"

"There'd be the jailors, you know, to chat with, and there's a yard to walk about. I never walked about a yard; and I believe prisoners always play cards—I never did. Grandmama objects to cards; but I should *have* to do it then; and then there's a prison-dress. I'm so fond of dress, and it would be a change for a child to wear a prison-dress. They keep us in ankle-short skirts, and no improvers; so we have very little change till we come out; but the prison-dress *would* be a change; and then I should have my hair cut some particular way. Do you know, Clarice, whether they do it round a basin?"

"Have you done, Olga?"

"Dear me, Clarice, no! I could go on for an hour longer, saying the same sort of things, if you like to listen."

"But I won't listen for another minute. Dear Olga, you make me very unhappy; do please be good, and write the letter when I beg you so. I am doing everything I can for you, and you really might do this one little thing for me."

"Oh, that's not fair. Of course I must do it now, if you put it that way—and it's very unfair; and you make me act on feeling, not principle, and you such a good girl! I'm astonished at you, Clarice—I really am. Well give us the pen and ink. Now, what am I to say?"

"Just the truth; tell her how unhappy you were, and how you ran away, and that you are hiding here and want her to write to Papa—"

"But I can't say that if I'm to tell the truth; for I don't, in the least, want her to write to your Papa."

"Very well—tell her to write to you then, and to tell you what you're to do; and you had better send her the advertisement, and say people here are watching for you, and that you are really in danger of being taken up and sent to prison if something is not done."

Olga began to laugh.

"It *is* such an idea, that I should be called a thief, and be sent to prison," said she; "it keeps on seeming as if it must be play. I don't get used to it a bit."

"And you had better tell her that a man saw you with the jewels, and picked up a pearl ring and a five-pound note."

"I can't say all that. Poor dear! she *would* fumble so."

"But it *is* so much better to tell the whole truth."

"And I don't write letters so easy as all that, Clarice; I can't go tearing on with my pen as I do with my tongue; it will take me nearly a fortnight to put down in a neat running hand—such as Grandmama would approve—all the things you have been saying."

"If it will take you so long, you had certainly better begin it at once, my dear."

"Very well, here goes!—isn't that vulgar, Clarice? I *did* learn to be vulgar at school—it was the only thing they taught *well*; there was a great big girl, with a cast in her eye, who used to say 'Here goes!' about everything. Can you get a cast in your eye if you try? How I have tried! I almost learnt that too, but not quite—it's much more difficult than being vulgar—you have to see your nose, and it's not at all easy to see your nose if it's such a little, wee nose as mine. Fanny had a fine large nose, sticking out just in the middle of her face, so she'd no merit in having a cast in her eye; but it would be great merit in me, because my nose is so little."

"Don't try to squint, dear; it would be a pity, and I don't think it would help you to write your letter."

"Well, here goes without the squint then."

"DEAREST GRANDMAMA,"

"There's a beginning for you at any rate."

"Olga has been very naughty and run away from school; but she *was* so unhappy there, and everything was shocking; she meant to go right away to Scotland and find you, but when she got out she found she had made a mistake, and was very nearly in London, so a darling dear girl is hiding her at ——"

"Now, Clarice, I shall leave a blank there, and you must write the name so that she can find me, for I can't write long strange names—it's as bad as doing a lesson."

"And now, Dearest Grandmama, will you write me a letter, and say you don't mind, and that I may come to you directly?—only, you must put

Aunt Jessie away somewhere, and I won't be in disgrace, you know; because, if you had been sent to that school, Grandmama, instead of me, you'd know how horrid it was, and you'd say it was quite, quite good of me to run away—gooder than bearing it—you would indeed. Somebody has put a wicked advertisement into the paper, saying I'm a thief; and a man has seen me and is watching to take me up, and has got my pearl ring and one of your five-pound notes; but my friend keeps on hiding me, and, if you are very quick indeed, you may get me before the man does. All the grown-up people, as usual, are wrong, and would do mischief, but, luckily, my friend is a child—"

"Are you a child, Clarice—is fifteen a child? May I call you one?"

"Oh, yes, you may call me one if you like."

"My friend is a child, and so knows what's right, and perhaps we two children may be able to keep me out of prison. Dearest Grandmama, don't be vexed, but be as quick as ever you can.

Your own loving

OLGA."

"The worst of Grandmama is that she is not quick. The fumbling slowers her very much, so it's best to chivy her a little bit, you know. I hope she won't mind, Clarice; I can't bear vexing Grandmama."

"I suppose," said Clarice, carefully reading it over, "I suppose that letter will do—she'll understand what has happened from it, I suppose."

Then she wrote her father's name and address in the blank, and pondered again as to whether there was anything more that ought to be said.

"I suppose it will do," she repeated, but rather doubtfully.

"It must do," replied Olga, "for I'm certainly not going to write another; I've got the cramp in two of my thumbs and all my toes as it is."

The letter was then done up, and directed—

"MRS LESLIE,
Glenkeen Castle,
———shire,
Scotland. To be forwarded."

"Now," said Clarice, "I shall take it and put it in the post-office myself. I dare not leave it to go with the other letters for fear anybody should notice it, and say anything about it."

"I wonder you were so determined to make me write it, if you are ashamed of it the minute it's done!"

Clarice laughed—her heart felt much lighter now this letter was written. It was the first step towards getting out of the labyrinth in which she had become involved, or as she did not hesitate to confess, had involved herself; and now the truth had been told to Olga's Grandmother, she did not feel so guilty in deceiving her own father. She was sure he would approve of this letter, and it was the first thing that had been done in the matter of which she did feel sure he would approve.

She implored Olga, in the most earnest manner, to keep in the cupboard while she was gone. "Remember," she said, "it is not like the other days—when, if you had been seen, no one would have known who you were; people are watching for you—the police are watching for you."

"It *must* be a judgment upon you for saying I was not like a real policeman," replied Olga; however, she promised that she would be very careful, and would not stir out of the closet till Clarice returned.

Clarice set off with her letter. She met Mr Linton on the road to the post-office, and hastily hid it under her mantle.

"I was coming to ask you to drink tea with us to-night," said he.

Drinking tea at the Parsonage was always a

great pleasure to Clarice, but she said now, "Oh! I am very sorry, but I can't come."

"I told your father last night, and he said you might."

"I am very sorry, Mr Linton, but it is impossible. I really can't come this evening."

"But why?—is it because Miss Simmonds is not well?—how is she to-day?"

Here was another temptation to say what was not true. It was dreadful to Clarice how she was now constantly feeling *tempted* to tell falsehoods; she who had always loved truth, and despised falsehood, so that the latter had seldom assumed the form of a *temptation* to her.

"She is better—it is not on her account, it is for another reason—but I can't come—please don't ask me."

Surprised at her agitated manner, Mr Linton looked at her earnestly. "They ought not to make you act as post this hot weather. You look fagged, and it is not good for you to be walking in this sunshine. Give me the letters and I will put them in the post."

"Thanks!" cried she, more agitated than ever—"but I must go on. I have things to do in the village. I must go myself. I like the walk. I do indeed."

"My dear Clarice, what is the matter with you?"

She burst into tears.

"Don't ask me," she said; "it is nothing, and it will be gone in a day or two."

"Now, Clarice, if there is anything the matter, you have plenty of friends, and you might confide in some of them. You always like a talk with my wife—come up to tea this evening—I'll be out of the way, and you shall have her to yourself."

"You are *very* kind to me," replied Clarice, "and I am *very* grateful, but I can't come."

"A wilful woman must have her way," said he, shrugging his shoulders, and they walked on in silence, for he had turned with her, and was also going to the village.

"By-the-by," said he, "you mustn't be alarmed if you find policemen prowling round your house, or standing in the garden or little wood. That man—Hughes is his name—has put the matter into their hands, and they are going to keep a watch on your house, and on mine, because the thief has been seen at both. They have telegraphed to the address given in the advertisement, saying that the girl is supposed to be here, and mentioning the ring and note, and asking for the numbers of the stolen notes by which this one can be identified; and they have ascertained no one answering to her description has left any of the railway stations, and there is now a watch on all, so I don't think the *soi-disant* Mrs Jennings can escape."

"What will they do with her if they take her?" said Clarice, gasping for breath.

"Put her in prison and try her for theft, I suppose; but I think a reformatory would be the best place for her, if she is really no more than fifteen."

Olga in a reformatory! Clarice could have laughed out loud at the idea, and then could have cried with equal abandonment, but she dared not do either, so with infinite effort she kept back both her laughter and her tears.

"I suppose the police can't come into our houses?" she said at last.

"No, not without a warrant, except in a case like this, you know; if they had reason to suppose the thief had concealed herself anywhere, they would come to your father, or to me, if it was at the Parsonage, and ask for leave to search the house, which, of course, would be granted them directly."

"Could you give up a person to justice, Mr Linton?"

"Could I?" said he laughing. "Yes, of course I could, and be very glad to do it too. If I had known about that little woman yesterday when she was giving me a taste of her impudence, I would have handed her over to the police with the greatest pleasure, and have thought I was doing her quite as great a favour personally, as I certainly was to society in general."

"And suppose she had been innocent?"

"If she was not the person meant in the advertisement, it would have been an annoyance to her for half-a-day, and then all would have come right."

"But if she *was* the person meant, and yet innocent?"

"But that is not possible, Clarice; if she is the person advertised for, she has absconded with the money and jewels, and *must* be guilty."

Clarice sighed heavily.

"It is very dreadful," said she.

"My dear girl, there is nothing dreadful about it; you are too sensitive. I declare, you are thoroughly put out, because you have been in the same room for five minutes with a thief; I don't know how you are to get through the world at all, at that rate."

"I believe, Mr Linton, that a great many people are supposed to be guilty who are innocent."

"Spoken like a sage, my dear Clarice, but I

believe *vice versa* of that also; and this girl can't very well be innocent. Look here! this advertisement is doubtless put in by the lady who keeps the school. A servant has run away, and money and jewels are missed, but unless there was undoubted proof that she had taken them, you may be quite sure such an advertisement would not have been inserted. And in this case there *is* no possible doubt, because the girl has actually been seen with the money and jewels in her possession, and has dropped some of both, which have been secured."

"Oh!" cried Clarice impatiently, "it is so easy to make anything seem as if it must be; anything can be described as if it was something else, and then can be described over again like itself, and nothing seem wrong or as if it wasn't."

"Well, I suppose you understand what you mean by that wonderful piece of argument, but I confess I don't; you are going quite beyond me now. Let me see. What is it? Everything is nothing at all, and everybody is somebody else. Was that what you said, Clarice?"

By this time they had reached the post-office, and Clarice, with a great sensation of relief, was going to slip her letter into the slit, when she suddenly discovered that she no longer held it concealed in the folds of her mantle. She had dropped it on the road!

"Oh! my letter, my letter," she cried, unable to conceal her distress. "I have lost my letter!"

"Never mind, we'll find it," said Mr Linton, good-naturedly. "Who is it for? What is it like?"

"It is just a common, white square letter, with a stamp on it," replied she, blushing violently, and hastily retracing her steps.

"Here, is this it?" cried he, picking something up. "'To Mrs Leslie, Glenkeen Castle, ——shire, Scotland.' I'm afraid it is not for you. I don't think you know any such person."

Clarice quietly took the letter from his hand, and without a word put it into the post-office.

"It is very odd," said Mr Linton, "but if you once see a name or a word you are sure to see the same thing over again directly; to the best of my belief I never heard the name of Leslie of Glenkeen Castle before to-day, and yet I am quite sure I saw something about it in the newspaper this morning, and now here it is again on a letter."

"What—what did you see about it in the paper?" said Clarice, trying to speak calmly.

"Oh, I don't know," answered he, "but I am sure I saw the name; it must have been among the births or deaths I suppose."

She stood still and got quite pale.

"Oh, not among the deaths, Mr Linton!" she cried piteously, "her Grandmama is not dead?"

"Whose Grandmama?"

"I don't know," she said in a very low voice. "I was thinking of someone—I was frightened—I can't quite exactly tell you—but do, please, try and recollect what you saw."

"Ah, I have it!" cried he, "and it was not among the deaths—and it was nobody's Grandmama. It was among the list of passengers from India by the *Melpomene*; the first name on the list was Colonel and Mrs Leslie of Glenkeen Castle—so your letter will hardly reach Mrs Leslie in Scotland, for it was only that they were at Marseilles on their way home."

"Oh, is that all?" said Clarice, and she drew a deep breath.

Soon after this Mr Linton bade her good-bye, and she went home as quickly as she could. A policeman stopped her at the door of her own house.

"I hope no offence, Ma'am," said he, "but do you think Mr Clavering would object to our going through the house; we are keeping strict watch on it, and we have reason to believe the girl we are looking for is inside. Can you trust all the servants, Miss?"

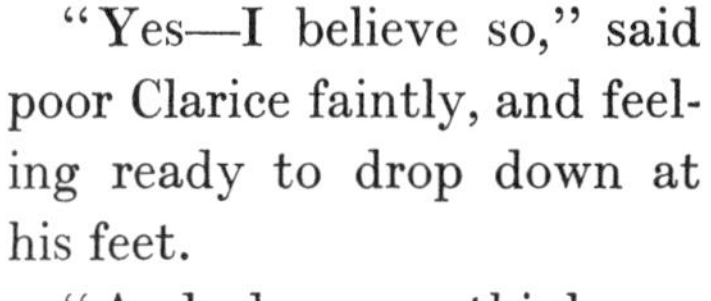

"Yes—I believe so," said poor Clarice faintly, and feeling ready to drop down at his feet.

"And do you think we might come in, Ma'am?"

"No—I'd rather not, please—not till Papa comes home; he'll be back soon, but I should not wish it till he comes."

Clarice could hardly command her lips and her tongue sufficiently to form these words, but by a violent exertion she succeeded in articulating, though she scarcely recognised the sound of her own voice.

The man looked rather disappointed. "Well, Ma'am, of course it must be as you please," he said; "but it might be important to come in at once."

"I am sure Papa would not like it in his absence," was all Clarice could find to say in reply. "I must ask you to wait till his return."

And so she entered the house, and flew upstairs to Olga.

"Oh, Olga!" she cried, "what will become of us? the police are to search the house!"

"Did they tell you so?" answered Olga.

"Oh yes, yes!"

"Have you been talking to a policeman, then?"

"Yes, I have."

"And did you guess him?"

"Guess him! what *do* you mean?"

"Why, you did not guess *me* when I was a policeman, so perhaps *this* was not one after all!"

Clarice took hold of her shoulder and gave her a little shake.

"Don't be tiresome!" she cried; "this is no time for it—the police are to search the house as soon as ever Papa comes home, if not before; I have begged them to wait till then, but I don't think they like it, and perhaps they will not mind what I've said, but will send up and ask Miss Simmonds. They think you are here. Have you been showing yourself, or doing anything foolish?"

"No," said Olga, reluctantly, "I've not been showing myself particularly."

"Why, what did you do?"

"Oh, not much—I *did* get out on the roof just for a very little while, but I'm sure nobody saw me; and if they had they would not have thought

it was me, for thieves never walk upon the roofs of houses in the daytime—it's too conspicuous."

"But what could make you do that?"

"I could not help it, Clarice; I found a ladder and a trap-door, so I *had* to go."

"Then, you must have been wandering about the house?"

"I did explore just a very little. I must explore a little bit every day, you know, or else how can I write travels? *Nobody* can write travels who does not explore. I'd do anything to please you, dear Clarice, but I *can't* write travels—not that will be worth reading at any rate—unless I explore—nobody could."

"But, Olga, I wonder whether you understand the meaning of words; I wonder whether you understand what I have been saying to you. I tell you the police are coming to search the house, and where can we possibly hide you that you will not be found?"

"Well, Clarice," replied Olga, in a meritorious tone of voice, "to please you, you know, I don't mind going into that closet for a *short* time, provided I have a candle and a story-book."

"You have not got a grain of common sense, Olga. Of course, if they search the house they'll look into cupboards and closets, and all those sort of places."

"Oh, they will, will they?" rejoined Olga composedly; "then they'll find *me*—I hope they'll like me!"

"Dear Olga, do be serious—do help me to think what can be done."

Olga clapped her hands, and began dancing.

"I know," cried she, "I know—I saw it just now when I was on the roof. There's the dearest little dumpty place among the chimneys, where a very small little thing like me can crouch up in a ball and nobody know—it will be delicious to be crumpled up there. Let me go, Clarice—don't hold me, dear Clarice—let me go—and you have the police in, this moment—stupid fellows—and set them hunting—they won't find me there—they never could, no—not if I cried "Whoop!" ever so loud."

"No, it wouldn't do," replied Clarice—"it wouldn't do at all—you might be seen getting up there, and all would be found out, unless it was after Papa came home, and was quite dusk," added she thoughtfully, "Then, perhaps, it might be done."

"It requires light to get to the dumpty place without rolling off the roof," said Olga coolly; "but I shall not mind that much—because I can climb like a cat, so I suppose I can tumble like a cat without being hurt—and if I can't I ought, and so it's quite right, that whoever didn't make me able to do it when I ought, should be punished by my coming to grief because I can't."

"Oh, Olga, there's no time for talking nonsense now; I can't *think* what we had better do."

"Will they search all over the house?" asked Olga.

"I suppose so—that is to say, wherever anybody could go without being noticed."

"But surely not in your bedroom?"

"I dare say not—if I had been here all day—but I have been out, which is very unlucky. Now, if I had been sitting here or in the library all the morning, very likely they would not care to search there."

"But that woman who screams at me, has been in her room all day," remarked Olga.

"Oh, Olga, how quick you are! of course she has, and of course it is in her room we must manage to hide you!"

"I'll stand opposite to her, and make signs at her all the time they're searching," said Olga. "I shan't mind that at all—it's very pleasant being a ghost."

"I had better go and see her at once," said Clarice, "and look about her room with a view to where you can be hid."

"But there's the dinner-bell," said Olga.

So Clarice went for a minute only to Miss Simmonds, to ask her how she was, and whether she could eat any dinner.

She was lying on the bed in her room, and said she thought she had now nothing at all the matter with her but a heavy cold, which made her head ache, and her eyes weak; and she asked Clarice to pull down the blind, and to send her up a little pudding for her dinner, as she would not take anything else.

"Of course you will not come down-stairs to-day," Clarice said, trembling with anxiety as to what the answer would be.

"Oh no, my love! I should not think of it; but to-morrow I expect to be about as usual. I hope you will have all that Italian and all that German quite ready for me."

"I hope so," replied Clarice, though in her own mind she felt it would not be possible for her to attend to lessons at present.

Then she looked about the room and made observations. There was no place where Olga could possibly conceal herself without crossing the foot of the bed, but when once that was done, there was a recess in the wall, with a curtain before it, that seemed as if it had been made on purpose. Clarice thought it might be managed thus. She would go into the room when the time drew near for the police to come; the servants would all be sure to be down-stairs to see what was going on; and then, while she drew off Miss Simmonds' attention by talking to her, Olga could slip in and get to the recess without being seen, and after the police had left the house she could be spirited out of the room in the same way. It would be quite dusk, so she hoped the whole thing might be managed without any difficulty.

Then she had to go down-stairs and eat her dinner, though anxiety and excitement had quite taken away her appetite. It was easy to purvey for Olga to-day, for, as she dined alone, she told Wilson not to wait.

She did nothing but calculate the days that must elapse before an answer to the letter came from Mrs Leslie. The post to the Highlands, she thought, must take two or three days, and then the letter would have to be forwarded somewhere else, and then the time for the answer to come. It seemed to her it could not arrive in less than a week, and how would it be possible for her to hold out against the besiegers for a whole week? and every whole week must have a Sunday in it—a Sunday, when she must leave Olga to herself during two long services, and when her Papa would be at home all day, and expect her to walk with him, and be his companion. Then Clarice suddenly remembered telegrams. Perhaps Mrs Leslie would send a telegram, and so shorten the time by half-a-week. How much more difficult it must have been to hide a king in the days when there were neither railways nor telegrams!

Chapter VIII

When Mr Clavering came home that evening, Clarice met him in the hall, and told him what the policeman had said.

"I know," replied he; "the fellow was at me about it when I drove up. It's utter nonsense—it's not possible anybody can be concealed in this house; the absurdity of the idea is on the face of it.

However, I don't like to refuse, so I've told them they may come after dinner. I'm not going to put off my dinner, and I'm not going to have them running over the house without me."

And so he went grumbling up-stairs to dress, and Clarice ran into her own room, where Olga was.

"We have till Papa has finished his dinner," she cried, "and then they are to come and go over the house. Oh! how my heart beats. Are you very much frightened, Olga?"

"No," replied Olga, "I don't mind policemen. I never did. I shall go into the screaming woman's room and be quite safe. I know they won't hurt me. I don't like *strange* dogs or *any* cows, but I never did mind policemen."

"Well, I am glad you are not frightened."

"Were *you* always afraid of them?"

"Of whom?"

"Why, policemen of course."

"No—why should I be? I'm not afraid of them now *as* policemen—only because they may find you."

"Ah—well—I'm afraid of cows *as* cows, and I thought you might have got a shock from a policeman some day, and that was why you were frightened. I never cared about cows, till one ran at my nurse when she was carrying me, ages ago;

but ever since that I have been *so* afraid of them. I suppose you never had a policeman run at you?"

"I declare, Olga, I think you seem to be always more foolish about policemen than about anything else—how very odd it is!"

"I was only trying to account for it, Clarice."

"Now, Olga, I am going to tell you something Mr Linton saw in the newspaper to-day."

"I think I had rather not hear it. I suppose it was another advertisement about Me?"

"No, indeed—it was something you will be very glad to hear."

"Make haste then, Clarice; tell me quick, can't you?"

"He saw in the paper that your father and mother had reached Marseilles on their way to England."

"Oh, Clarice!" and Olga's cheeks grew as pink as the roses that peeped in at the window, and two great tears fell out of her blue eyes upon them.

Clarice kissed her. "I think, dear, they will be in London in a day or two—do you know where they will stay?"

"At the Grosvenor Hotel, I suppose—that is where they were before. Don't you think I'd better go up there—I mean, of course, as soon as the police are gone?"

"No, a child like you couldn't go to a hotel by herself; but you'd better write there—or if we knew how to do it we might send a telegram—but at any rate, you might write by to-morrow's post, for if it seemed very desirable we could send the telegram afterwards at any time."

"No," said Olga, shaking her head, "*that* wouldn't do. I know nothing about it. I couldn't work the wires, and I don't understand the language—and I don't *like* telegrams either—they're so abrupt, it's quite rude—just, so and so, to such a one, and then a few scattered words, put in columns, as if they were trying to be sums, and with dashes between them, though they are always only one sentence, and all the little words left out, and I like the little words best. No, Clarice, I won't send a telegram."

"Well, you will write a letter then, of course?"

"Yes, I'll write a letter, and I only hope it will do Papa good, and that he'll see what a foolish, foolish thing it was to send me to school. I told him so; but if you'll believe me, Clarice, it made no more impression on him than if he'd been a kitten. Do you find your Papa *very* troublesome sometimes?"

"I'm afraid I shall about you, Miss Olga," replied Clarice, smiling, but giving a little impatient sigh at the same time; "I am sure he will be greatly displeased at all I have done."

"He'll get over it," said Olga, coolly; "they do if you let them quite alone, and take no notice."

"There's the hall-bell!" cried Clarice, with a great start. She went to the door of her room, opened it, peeped out, and listened, then came back to Olga and said softly, "Now, come with me—we will go along the passage and into her room together—then you remain by the door while I go up to the bed and talk to her, and when she begins to answer me, you steal very softly by the foot of the bed, and run behind the curtain, which you will see just opposite you as you walk along. There you must stay till the search is over, and we hear the hall door shut behind them, and then you may come out and get very quietly out of the room again."

"You will have to give me some sign when I am to do that."

"Very well, I will bid her good-night and then you may come."

"I wish it was over; but I should be *much* more uncomfortable if it was a couple of cows that were coming to look for me—so it might be worse."

The two girls stole along the passage, and distinguished as they did so that there were people in the hall below them.

"People," whispered Olga to her terrified companion, who dragged her breathlessly along when she found her beginning to talk—"people, *not* cows!"

They entered Miss Simmonds' room, Olga remaining by the door, in obedience to Clarice's instructions, while she herself went up to the bedside.

"You were not asleep? I did not wake you?"

"No, I was only lying with my eyes shut, I had tired them by reading. I am very glad to see you, my dear—have you finished that German translation?"

"Not yet," replied Clarice, with a sigh.

"You must not be idle, Clarice, because I am not able to teach you for a day or two; you are old enough to do a great deal by yourself now."

As she spoke, a frightened look came into the good governess's eyes, and she interrupted herself by a little exclamation as if in pain. Clarice, yielding to an impulse too strong to be resisted, put her hand down over her eyes.

"Don't mind it," she cried, "it is nothing—it is not that you are ill—it is something I will explain to you very soon. I can't *bear* you to be frightened, and fancying yourself ill."

"My dear," said the unimaginative lady, "what do you mean? how is it possible you can explain it? Don't vex yourself, dear—I am better, though not quite well yet."

Olga had reached the recess, and Clarice withdrew her hand. Miss Simmonds glanced wearily at the foot of the bed, and then gave a sigh of relief.

Then Clarice went softly out of the room.

"I will be back in a minute," she said.

When she came into the passage, she found her father and the policemen in the act of leaving her own room, of which they had made a slight passing inspection. "In course the occupied rooms are not likely to be selected," one of the men was saying to her father.

"You will not come in here," said she, gently, keeping guard on the door; "there is a sick lady here who has been in bed all day."

"Oh no, Miss! in course not," said the men, and they passed on with her father, while she re-entered Miss Simmonds' apartment. To her horror, the first thing she saw was Olga standing before the looking-glass brushing out her hair into a halo, and making grimaces at the reflected image of her fair little face in the mirror. Miss Simmonds had her back turned to her, but lay in bed so as to be facing Clarice, in consequence of which the latter did not dare make even the slightest sign to Olga to bid her return to the recess, while Olga, seeing Clarice in the glass, made horrible grimaces at her, laughing and nodding her head up and down, triumphant in her own disobedience and in Clarice's helpless condition.

"What is that noise in the house, my dear?" asked the governess.

"Some men whom Papa is taking to look at something."

"Oh! workmen, I suppose," said the unimaginative one, quite contented to receive anything she might be told, without inquiry.

How impatiently Clarice longed for them to go away! How she desired to get Olga out of the room, and have her safely locked up in her cupboard. She kept Miss Simmonds in chat, so as to make her still turn towards her, and dreaded each moment lest she should become restless and turn round the other way. She almost screamed when at last she found Miss Simmonds making little movements, half-raising herself up, and preparing to lie on her back—but Olga saw this too in the looking-glass, and, quick as thought, darted behind the curtain before she was perceived. Then Clarice breathed freely again, for she saw that Olga, notwithstanding the spirit of mischief that possessed her, did not mean to be seen; and her great object was that Miss Simmonds should not be frightened. It seemed so cruel to make the good, patient woman suffer, that Clarice never felt her task so difficult, or was so much tempted to say something that would betray Olga, as at those moments.

"Did you cover the last sets of tracts that Mr Linton gave you, Clarice?" asked Miss Simmonds presently.

"No, indeed, I did not. I quite forgot all about it; but I will, if I can only recollect it."

"You should try to remember these sort of things. You are not a child now, and you could be of a great deal of use in little matters. I am afraid you are being idle because I am ill. Now that is just the very reason why you should try to be more thoughtful, and to do more than usual."

Clarice received the reproof in silence. She saw that her conduct had laid her open to all that Miss

Simmonds said, and she could not explain. Then, fearing lest her governess should imagine her sullen because she did not speak, she simply said, "I will try."

"That is right, my dear girl—that is better than making too many promises; but, Clarice, if you really try you will undoubtedly succeed. However, I hope after to-morrow, perhaps, I shall be as usual—but you should do all the lessons you can just the same now as if I was with you; and one thing surprises me very much, I have not heard the piano once since I was ill—why don't you practise, my dear?"

Clarice was silent.

"It would not disturb me in the least—are you afraid lest it should disturb me?"

Then Clarice did what was most unusual to her. She gently kissed Miss Simmonds' forehead. She did not know when she had ever done such a thing before, as offer a caress to that lady, whose manners and ways were not such as to invite caresses; but she could not help it now. She had a sort of conscience-stricken feeling, though she hardly knew why. "I will make a point of practising to-morrow," she said.

The difficulty of not saying what was untrue, while the concealment of Olga lasted, perfectly appalled Clarice. She felt very thankful that this difficulty had presented itself to her so very early in the affair that she had been much on her guard—for she confessed that had it not been so, she must have been betrayed into falsehood. She also saw that if she had been younger, and so less able to reflect, she must several times have been hurried into an untruth, if only by agreeing to the reasons for her conduct, suggested to her by others; and she felt keenly how right it was that children never should conceal anything from their parents, but be open as the day, and frank and confiding in all their dealings. She also reproached herself for too much confidence in her own judgment, and acknowledged that if she had had more humility, she never would have been placed in this position; and while these reflections were passing through her mind, it occurred to her that even at this very moment she might be deceiving Miss Simmonds, who possibly accepted her kiss as a tacit admission that she *had* abstained from practising on her account.

So she said, hurriedly, "It was not for fear of disturbing you that I did not practise."

"Oh, very well, my dear," was the reply, "but I am sorry you have not been more regular and industrious ,and I hope you will try to be so in future."

Then she closed her eyes and seemed tired, and Clarice felt how odd her staying on must appear, and how much more natural it would be, that she should bid her good-night and leave her.

At last she heard voices in the hall.

"People, not cows," she said to herself mechanically, repeating Olga's words without reflecting on the meaning—"People, not cows."

The house door shut with a great bang, and then the drawing-room door, so she knew her father had gone in there, and would soon expect her to join him and make his tea.

"Well, you are tired, and I had better say good-night," she said, in a marked manner that made Miss Simmonds suddenly open her eyes. "Don't move—shut your eyes again and go to sleep," and she stooped her head again while she spoke, in front of Miss Simmonds' face, so as to conceal from her the figure of Olga, whom she had the satisfaction of knowing was stealing undiscovered from the room.

"Now I will go," she said.

But who could reckon upon Olga for, as Clarice had herself said, half-a-minute together? Perhaps she was disappointed at Clarice having succeeded in preventing Miss Simmonds from seeing her, after she had brushed out her golden curls, into such a remarkably stiff halo—perhaps she only yielded

to one of those sudden impulses which sometimes appeared to be the mainspring of her conduct—be it as it may—from whatever reason it proceeded, what she did was this—she paused one moment on the threshold ere she closed the door behind her, and in loud, sweet, piercing tones shouted out "Whoop, tally ho!"

Imagine the astonishment of Miss Simmonds! Imagine the horror and rage of Clarice! "What was it?" cried the sick woman, as if there could be the slightest doubt what it was.

"It was some one said 'Whoop, tally ho!'" replied Clarice, speaking gravely and distinctly; for her fear was, lest her poor friend should think that fever had seized on her senses, and that she was hearing voices as well as seeing visions.

She made the statement in a quiet, commonplace way, as if there was nothing remarkable in the fact.

"But how odd!" said her governess. She was not an excitable woman, or one much given to wonder; but it *did* seem odd to her.

"Good-night, Miss Simmonds!" said Clarice.

"But, dear Clarice, stop a minute! Who *could* say 'Whoop, tally ho!' in my room, or in fact, anywhere?"

She meant anywhere in the house, but the strangeness of the circumstance had confused her, and she did not use her usually perspicuous language.

"It's *not* a difficult thing to say," replied Clarice vaguely and gently.

"But you don't seem surprised; you seem hardly to take in what has happened," remonstrated her governess—"it is so very unusual, and somebody *must* have done it."

"Yes!" agreed Clarice; and then neither of them said any more.

"I think," Miss Simmonds said at last, sinking back among her pillows, from which in her surprise she had half-raised herself; "I think, my dear, you had better ask the servants."

"Yes!" cried Clarice eagerly, and then suddenly felt *that* was not true. "It is frightful," she said to herself, "how every first word that comes to my lips is false! I *don't* mean to ask the servants"; so she blushed, and stammered, and corrected herself into saying, "I will speak very severely to whoever said it—that I promise you."

"Yes, if you find out who it was; but who *could* it be? I can't think of anybody in the house who would do such a thing. Who were those people you said your Papa was taking about?"

"People, not cows!" murmured Clarice, as the word "people" reached her ear without making an impression on her mind, and then could have beaten herself for her folly.

"I don't know their names," was her answer aloud; "but it is nearly tea-time, and I am not dressed. I *must* leave you now."

"Oh yes, you must not keep your Papa waiting! You must never be unpunctual, my dear!—punctuality is the root of so many virtues. 'Whoop, tally ho!' how *very* odd!"

And she settled herself in the bed as she spoke, and Clarice hastily and gladly made her escape from the room.

She flew to her own apartment, and accosted Olga really angrily: "Olga, how could you?—it was very, very wrong. Will you never understand that you owe something to people who are assisting you?"

"I could not help it, Clarice—it was because she did not see me."

"Such nonsense! when you knew the great object was that she shouldn't see you."

"No, *indeed*, it wasn't, Clarice; it couldn't be. I had haloed my hair on purpose."

"You are too silly, Olga!"

"But then why did I halo my hair?—that proves it, you know; and you havn't the least bit of proof to offer on your side. *You* have only assertion."

"Olga, if you will only listen to me—"

"I had *much* rather not, dear Clarice! Assertion, without proof, is nothing."

"You have done exceedingly wrong, Olga—I can tell you that—and got us into a great difficulty. I don't see how *that*—" (Clarice could not bring herself to say the words "Whoop, tally ho!") "is to be explained away."

"Then why did you not let her see me?"

"Because that was the thing I was most anxious to prevent."

"There it is, you see, Clarice—since she didn't see me, I had to say, 'Whoop, tally ho!' What else was there for me to do? I couldn't help myself!"

"Very well, Olga, I have nothing more to say. You will be sorry for all this some day."

"Good gracious! Clarice, that's just exactly what Mrs Jennings used to say; and if a girl was so foolish as to admit that she *was* sorry for anything, and some of them were rather shabby, and didn't mind, she'd always reply, 'So am I.' Wasn't that nasty?"

Clarice began to dress, and arrange her hair in silence, and vouchsafed no answer to Olga's last question.

"Clarice, I don't like to vex you," said the little maiden; "I'll go into her room directly and unsay it, if that'll satisfy you."

"What do you mean by unsaying it, pray?"

"Why, I'll give a wail, or I'll cry like a hunted hare, and then I'll moan out in a miserable, miserable manner—no whoop! no tally ho!—will that do, Clarice?"

"Olga, you are enough to tire the patience of Job; but there is no being angry with you for five minutes together. You are too foolish, in fact, for it to be worth while being angry with you."

Olga clapped her hands, as she was so fond of doing, and danced about the room crying out, "It is so nice to be a fool."

"That's a pleasure," said she presently, "that you and your Miss Simmonds will never know."

"What pleasure is that?"

"Why, being a fool, of course. Sensible people have not an idea how much they lose!"

"Perhaps fools have not an idea how much they lose either."

"Oh, yes, they have. They can look up and see how horrid it is. Anybody can look up and see how small and silly, things seem high up in the air—little bits of things with nothing round them, and no reason for their being there. But you can't look down, because it makes you giddy—giddy—giddy—and so you have not the least little bit of a notion how pleasant it is, or how firm and satisfactory, to be a real fool."

"I wonder where you learned all your ideas, Olga."

"One doesn't learn ideas—does one? One learns lessons, but there never are any ideas in *them*. One hatches ideas, I suppose—not learns them."

"Hatches ideas?"

"Yes! the eggs come somehow or nohow into our minds, and then out of them fly the nice little birds, whether we want them or no."

"I sometimes think you're very clever, Olga."

Olga laughed, and fixed her innocent, childish blue eyes on Clarice. "I think it's such nonsense about being clever or stupid—that's what they were always boring on at, at school. We're *ourselves*, and what does it signify?"

"We're *ourselves*," repeated Clarice thoughtfully; "people, not cows!"

Olga burst out laughing. "Yes!" said she. "I often *am* glad of that—that cows only come now and then, on a road or in a lane—they're worst in a lane; but if they came everywhere, like people, what *should* we do?"

The clock struck.

"There's my signal," said Clarice. "I must go down to Papa."

"Give my love to the old gentleman, and tell him to keep up his spirits."

Then Clarice made Olga go into the cupboard, and locked the door on her.

"It's not for long," she said; "but I shall take away the key. I can't trust you to-night."

"Whoop, tally ho!" murmured Olga faintly through the key-hole.

CHAPTER IX

"There never was anything so foolish," grumbled Mr Clavering, while Clarice poured out his tea; "there never was anything so foolish as searching a man's house, in which it is *impossible* anybody should be concealed."

"Why did you let them do it, Papa?"

"My dear, if I had refused, they could have got a warrant. But the idea is preposterous—a moderate-sized house like this, full of people, and in a thickly populated country—the idea of anyone being concealed in it without the residents in the house finding them out! I'd defy the cleverest thief in London to hide in my house without my detecting him."

"Would you, Papa?"

"Yes, my dear, I would—but I'll tell you what, Clarice. I shall have my eye on that tall policeman. I doubt his being sober. I doubt his being strictly sober. I could not take upon myself to say that he was the least the worse for liquor when I saw him, but his cock-and-bull stories which have been at the bottom of all the disturbance look very like it. He's been seeing or hearing of this girl being seen, everywhere—in the garden—among the bushes—crossing the windows inside the house—and, if you'll believe me, on the roof. You were watched out of the house to the village, and he ascertained there was no other girl in the establishment, and then, forsooth, he sees one on the roof—a likely place for anybody who was hiding to go to in broad daylight. I wonder he was not ashamed to bring me such a story as *that*."

"I hope, Papa, we shall have no more worry from the policemen."

"No, my dear, I hope not—but it's impossible to say—people are so very obstinate when they have taken up an idea, and I don't trust that tall policeman one bit."

"Clarice," said her father presently, "why did not you drink tea with Mrs Linton to-night?"

"I did not feel inclined," stammered she, colouring a good deal.

"But that is very odd. You generally are inclined—and your refusal must have seemed rather ungracious after I had said you might go. It must have surprised them a little, I think."

"I am sorry, Papa, and I will certainly go the next time they ask me."

"Linton is not a touchy man, but with some people you might not be asked again in a hurry."

"I don't think he was at all put out with me, Papa; he is very good-natured."

As she spoke, the door was dashed open so violently that Clarice rose affrighted from her chair, with the word "Olga" on her lips, for she thought it could be no one but Olga who made an entrance after such a fashion. But to her great surprise it was not Olga, but Ann—Ann in a state of even greater terror and rage, than on the evening when she believed she had seen a spirit.

"I won't abear it, and I can't abear it," cried she. "Mr Clavering, Sir, as you're a gentleman, I swear, that wages or no wages I leaves your service this night!"

"What's the matter now, Ann?" inquired her master.

"Matter?" said she with scorn. "Yes, Sir, you can call it matter if you please—you're a gentleman, and I'm only a servant—but to *my* mind it's something more than matter. In Miss Clarice's hanging-closet there's the ghost of a hoss!"

"Of a what?"

"A hoss, Sir! it neighed at me three times, and it pawed the boards, and kicked, and trotted up and down, and neighed again. I knowed it," continued she, in great agitation. "Oh, yes, I knowed it directly. It's the ghost of a hoss my brother sent to the knackers—he didn't ought to have done it, my brother didn't. I knows he didn't ought—but was it my fault, and should the hoss haunt *me*? It was an old hoss, too, and should have knowed better than *that*!"

"You are a very foolish woman, Ann," said her master, "and if I did not know you well I should think you had been drinking—but I see you are quite sober, extremely foolish, and very much frightened. Did you look into the closet and *see* the horse?"

"*I*, Sir? *I* go near the creature—no, indeed, Mr Clavering. I *may* be only a servant, Sir, but I values myself more than *that*."

"Very well, come along with me, and we will open Miss Clarice's closet, and prove to your satisfaction that there is nothing worse there than a few dresses. Come with us, Clarice—we won't invade your premises without you."

Clarice was pale, and trembled a good deal.

"Oh, Sir, don't mind Ann's nonsense."

"No—no—we have too much of this sort of thing going on in the house—we shall have no peace unless we put a stop to it at once. Come, my dear, when I tell you, and let us show Ann how foolish she is."

Mr Clavering walked up-stairs, followed by the woman and the girl, both looking very much scared and frightened. Indeed, Clarice's heart beat so fast that she could hardly ascend the broad, easy flight of stairs. "Now," said he, when he had reached his daughter's bedroom. "Now, then, let us open this cupboard at once, and find the horse that has made such a mistake as to haunt Ann instead of her brother."

He tried to open the cupboard door.

"It is locked," he said. "Did you lock it, Ann? Give me the key."

"It's not me that locked it, Sir," replied Ann, "nor no one at all—it's a place that nobody ever *did* lock—nor never will, or I'm much mistaken."

"Give me the key, Clarice."

No answer.

"Have you got the key, Clarice, or where is it?"

Still Clarice made no reply; she stood supporting herself on the back of a chair, pale and trembling.

Mr Clavering turned round on her very impatiently. "Do you hear me? Surely you are not such an idiot as to be frightened at what Ann says. Give me the key this moment."

Clarice began looking vaguely about her as if searching for the key. "The key?" she said, in a confused aimless way.

"Yes, the key," replied he sharply; "pray don't keep me waiting in this absurd manner—do you think I have nothing better to do than to stand before this cupboard door, dancing attendance on the ghost of a horse?"

As the words passed his lips a low whinnying neigh was heard inside the closet. Mr Clavering jumped back a yard, giving utterance to the rather homely phrase, "Bless my heart!" Ann gave a loud piercing scream, and Clarice sank on the chair as if she had lost the power of standing, and covered her face with her hands.

At that moment there was a hasty knock at the

room door, and one of the house-maids entered. "A telegram, Sir!" she said, and handed Mr Clavering a paper.

Astonished as he was, a telegram is a thing that, as a business man, he could not fail to attend to—indeed, a telegram claims attention from every one; even those intolerable people who turn a letter round and round before opening it, treat a telegram with more respect. There are few hearts that do not beat a little quicker at the receipt of a telegram. Mr Clavering changed colour when he opened his. "My brother!" he exclaimed. "Clarice, your Uncle is very ill—I must run up to London by the next train." He looked at his watch. "I have just time to catch it—it is most important I should see him—there are business matters still unsettled which *cannot* be delayed—I will be back to dinner to-morrow." He gave her a hasty kiss. "I have no time to take anything with me—I will walk on, and you must send William after me with my bag."

"As to that horse," he added suddenly, recollecting what had occupied them the moment before—"it is *impossible*, you know, that it can be anything—but let Wilson examine the place, and you can sleep in the chintz room if you like. It *must* have been the wind or something—it *could* be nothing else." With which clear expression of opinion Mr Clavering made a hasty retreat.

Clarice knew her Uncle but little. He had for a long time been a great invalid, subject to sudden accessions of illness, and she was too young to feel anxious or alarmed. "Poor Uncle is ill again and wants to see Papa," was all she thought about it; then she told Ann she might go away.

"But the cupboard, Miss—the hoss?" said Ann.

"Oh, it is nothing," replied Clarice impatiently; "I am not afraid—do go away, Ann, and don't worry me any more."

"You don't mean to say, Miss, you are going to sleep in this room with only a plank between you and it."

"Yes, I am—I know it's nothing. Oh, Ann, do go away."

"It's a temptin' of Providence, Miss Clarice!"

"It's just a trick, Ann, and I know what made the sound though you don't. It's not a horse, or a ghost, or anything but a trick."

"It's a ghostly trick, Miss, then, and you'd better have nothin' to say to them sort of tricks."

"Oh, Ann, do go away."

"I'm gone, Miss Clarice, but if you'll take my advice, Miss, you'll go too, and not mix yourself up with them sort of unnatural craytures, whether they *be* tricks or baint."

Clarice gently pushed Ann out of the room, and locked the door upon her; then she took her key, unfastened the cupboard door, and in a very stern voice desired Olga to "Come out."

Olga obeyed—but how? A little white ball came rolling into the room, and up to Clarice's feet, where it unrolled itself, and then crumpled itself up again about them, and began kissing and stroking them, and saying, "I couldn't help it, Clarice—I can't help it, Clarice—Oh, Clarice, I am so sorry—but when I *can't* help it what am I to do?"

Clarice had only lately been a child herself, and did not find it easy to keep up the severity of her demeanour towards her offending little friend; and when she remembered the neigh that she had heard within the cupboard, and the effect that it had produced on her father, she found it impossible to restrain her laughter, which so enchanted the penitent ball at her feet, that it jumped up, and, unfolding itself on her knee, perched there, and began kissing her with dainty little kisses, as a bird might with its beak peck sugar from her lips.

In this manner they were reconciled, and Olga escaped the scolding she most certainly deserved.

"I do pity your Grandmama, if you go on in this way all day at Glenkeen Castle."

"Oh, but I don't, Clarice; it's only here, you know, because I'm pent up. You've no notion of the effect that being in there" (pointing to the cupboard) "has on one; and then I don't belong to anybody; I'm not one of the family; I'm altogether pent up, and I *have* to play tricks or else I should forget who I am; and, then, as nobody else knows it, I might really be lost."

"Well, I've got something for you to do to-night. It's too early to go to bed, and you must write to your father. It will never do for him to pass through London and go to Scotland without knowing about you. It's quite possible he's in London now, and if your letter goes by the early post he may get it to-morrow morning."

"I don't particularly want to write to Papa. I've nothing to say to him."

"Oh yes, indeed, you have! You must explain

to him that you are here and in trouble, and want him to come and fetch you."

"I'll tell him to come down in full Highland costume. I say, Clarice, is your Papa particularly old?"

"I don't quite know what you mean. I don't suppose he is particularly old."

"He did walk so heavily, and he spoke so grumpy. Is he grumpy, Clarice?"

"A little—sometimes—not very—not more than all gentlemen are now and then, you know."

"*My* Papa never is; and he walks as light—as light as a reindeer. He *couldn't* stump and flop as your Papa did, not if he tried ever so much."

"I don't consider that Papa does stump and flop, and I like a man to walk with dignity and weight," said Clarice, annoyed.

"Not stump and flop! Oh Clarice, and I heard him through the wall! and he puffed—I heard him puff—if you could only hear how *my* Papa breathes!"

"You would employ yourself much better if you would write to your Papa instead of boasting about him," replied Clarice, very sharply. "My Papa is a clever man, and has a name in the city"—poor Clarice, was this the conclusion of all her romance? but she was driven to her wits' end to find something to say in defence of her father, whom she really loved—"and nobody would *think* of noticing how he breathed."

"I daresay not, in the city," replied Olga calmly.

"Now Olga, do you mean to write to Colonel Leslie or do you not?"

"No, Clarice, I don't mean to do it."

"But you must."

"Oh very well, then; why did you ask me? I don't *mean*, but I must."

"If you write at once I can send it by the early post."

"I shall make it *very* short."

"Just as you like; only you must tell him enough to enable him to understand, and beg him to come down here the minute he gets your note."

Olga took the pen and paper Clarice gave her. She had not the pen of a ready writer any more than many other girls of her age, and she thought it a very inhuman thing to be forced to write two letters on the same day, but she saw that Clarice was in earnest, so that she should have to do it in the end, and that therefore she had better make up her mind to do it in the beginning with a good grace. Accordingly she wrote as follows:

"Darling Papa,

"I have run away from that horrid school and come to here, where I am in great trouble, for they say I am a thief, and want to put me in prison. They saw me on the roof of the house. The advertisement says that I stole Grandmama's jewels and money. I am very happy on the whole; but Clarice says you had better come down here at once, because she can't go on hiding me; and when you come you can explain everything to everybody. Darling Papa, *could* you come in Highland costume?

"Your loving little daughter,

"OLGA."

Clarice added the address, but she expressed a good deal of dissatisfaction with the note; she thought it would only puzzle Colonel Leslie, and that he could not understand it at all; and she said that her request about the Highland costume was simply ridiculous, and what *could* he suppose she meant about being seen on the roof?

However, Olga stoutly refused to say anything further, still more to write another note.

"I've told him in my own way," she said, "and if I didn't he wouldn't think it was me—and I *was* seen on the roof."

So Clarice put the note in the bag with the other letters to go early in the morning.

"At any rate," she said, "it will make him come down here, and that's the great thing. You can explain to him when he comes."

"I've told him that *he* is to explain," replied Olga.

"Yes, that was so absurd," said Clarice.

"No it wasn't," retorted Olga; "it was *much* the best thing I *could* have said to him."

"I wish he was here," sighed Clarice, "and all this trouble and concealment over. I don't think I shall ever wish for an adventure again."

"I'm sure," replied Olga, "I shall always run away from school again, whenever they put me there. I thought it would be nice, but it's nicer than nice. You see I couldn't imagine I should find *you*. Why, I might have gone on all my life till I was inconceivably old—as old as your Papa—without ever finding you, or knowing even that you were anywhere that could be found, if I hadn't run away from school. It's very odd indeed, Clarice, that more girls don't do it."

"I think it's time to go to bed now, Olga."

"Is it really too late for me to have a run down to the village and look in at the Parsonage?" asked Olga.

"I advise you to keep out of Mr Linton's way. He's very good-natured if we're good, but he's as sharp as a needle, and determined to have his own way, when he knows it's right."

"What will he say, then, when he finds out who his visitor was?"

"I don't exactly know; but I do know I'd rather not have been his visitor, for he won't be pleased."

"Well, that can't be helped. One can't always keep them pleased, you know; and clergymen especially are rather troublesome sometimes; but, as I said before, the best plan is to take very little notice."

Then the two girls went to bed.

The next day Miss Simmonds was better, but said she did not think she should come down-stairs till tea-time. Clarice avoided being with her, she was so afraid of her saying anything about the "Whoop, tally ho!" of the night before; but it seemed as if her governess thought it better not to speak to her on the subject. The first thing in the morning, she mentioned that she wished to see Mr Clavering, and was surprised to hear he had left home, and grieved at the cause. She looked anxious and perplexed, but was relieved by finding he would be back to dinner, and begged that he might be told she wished to speak with him immediately on his return.

Olga said that, as they had the house to themselves, there could be no reason why she should be kept up-stairs like a bedstead, and so she would settle herself in the library with Clarice. The latter reflected a good deal as to the safety and wisdom

of this proceeding, but at last decided that, with certain precautions, they might venture on the experiment. The library windows looked out on the flower-garden, which was quite private. In it they could distinctly hear any arrival at the hall door on the other side of the house, and there was a cupboard in the wall for maps and papers into which Olga could quite easily get if the danger was imminent. So in the library they took up their quarters, and both enjoyed the change and the freer feeling, they somehow or other experienced.

"I suppose," Olga said, "those police creatures have taken themselves off now, and will torment us no more."

"No," said Clarice, "that's what puzzles me. They are still watching the house from the road, and two of them are at the end of the lane by the glade, so indeed, Olga, it is impossible for you to be too careful."

"I don't suppose Papa and Mama *can* be in London yet," said Olga. "It's lucky I didn't go towards India, for I might have missed them after all."

"I don't know what I shall do without you, Olga, when they take you away, I've got so *used* to you, Olga."

"Yes, but we shall always be friends, and you'll come and see me at Glenkeen, and I shall pay you visits here, and we'll be each other's bridesmaids—that's what the girls at school always promised each other. Oh Clarice, how odd it is that all this will not be happening soon, and that some day we shall talk it over, and say to each other, do you remember this? and, do you remember that? I think that is the very oddest thing in life, Clarice. I never can fancy it at the time: it always seems to me that whatever is happening must go on, and that *we* can't go on, out of it."

"Yes," said Clarice, "I know what you mean; only I have always felt so desperately about things changing, and that they *must* change. When I was a child I loved my doll so. Oh how I did love her! I used to think of her the last thing at night and the first thing in the morning, and plan everything I did through the day with a view to her; and some of the most miserable moments I ever spent have been those in which I felt that when I grew up I should not care for her. It seemed to me such a fearful thing that I should actually cease to care for what then made my chief happiness. It used to embitter the great joy I had in my doll, and I have cried, only from the thought, that when I grew up I actually should cease to think about her."

"Then you come round to my plan of having only children in the world; for then you would not have grown up, and we should not have any of those inhuman changes."

"Now, I am going to write my German translation. I must not neglect it, Olga, and you must hold your tongue," said Clarice.

Olga took down a story-book from the shelves, and Clarice set to work at her lessons in a very conscientious manner.

Chapter X

They spent their time very comfortably till the afternoon, when Clarice was obliged to go into the garden to gather some flowers, as she knew her father would be displeased, if he found she had not refreshed the faded bouquets in the drawing-room. She dared not take Olga with her; and at first she proposed that she should go into her room during her absence, but to that the little maiden strongly objected; and, on reflection, Clarice agreed that there might be less danger in remaining quietly in the Library than would attend the journeys up and down stairs.

"But you really must be as still as a mouse," said she, "unless you hear a step in the hall, and then instantly take shelter in the cupboard."

"But when you are gone, I suppose I may dance a little?" replied Olga.

"Dance?" repeated Clarice in dismay.

"Yes, *dance*!" reiterated Olga, laying rather a dogged emphasis on the word. "Of course I said *dance*; what else *can* I do when I'm quite alone? Why, even a mouse does *that*!"

"Does it?" questioned Clarice, very doubtfully.

"Oh dear, yes!" replied Olga with decision, "always, and sings too. Did you never hear of singing mice? But of course I won't sing—that's noisy, and I'm far too reasonable to wish it; but you might let me dance, dear Clarice! just a very little."

"Well, perhaps," said Clarice, "a very little, and *very* quietly."

"Oh, so quietly!" replied Olga—"on tiptoe—in a whisper—under my breath."

And she began dancing as a fairy in a state of somnambulism, might dance, in a spectacle on the stage.

"That's quite safe—now, isn't it?" she said pleadingly. Clarice shook her head at her, and said she must not do it with one atom more spirit than that, and then she ran out into the garden.

On that lovely July afternoon, in an English garden full of roses, there was no difficulty in finding flowers to make a drawing-room pretty. Clarice almost doubted whether she would gather anything *but* roses, when she had filled her basket with the splendid creatures—purple, damask, crimson, pink, blush, yellow, and white—such a variety in shape and colour, and yet all the same flower. She buried her face in their fresh fragrance with a sensation of delight, and a quick wish that they themselves received as much pleasure from their beauty as they gave to others. Perhaps they do, she thought; they surely must, and their delicious scent is their way of thanking God for making them so beautiful. It is what music is to us—it is a hymn. And then she kissed the roses, she felt so thankful to them for singing such a sweet hymn.

With slow, happy steps she went back into the Library, her hands full of fairy treasures, which she placed with tender touch on a marble table.

"Come and help me arrange them, Olga," she said.

There was no reply, and she looked round, only to discover that Olga was not there.

"Oh!" she cried, "it is too bad; it is like a nightmare. I cannot leave her for a moment, or trust her for a moment. She will get into some dreadful scrape, just when all was growing happy, and a good end to the troubles close at hand!"

Then, with sudden hope, she opened the cupboard of maps. Olga might have heard her step in the hall, and not sure who it was, have concealed herself according to their agreement.

Alas, no! Olga was not there.

"Why should I distress myself so much about her?" argued Clarice with herself. "After all, it is only she that is concerned; and if she is so very naughty and mischievous she ought to suffer"; but she sighed even as she said it, for she knew she could not cast Olga off if she tried, and must suffer for and with her.

Just then she heard a scuffling, rushing sound in the hall, the door opened suddenly, and in flew Olga, breathless, flushed, frightened.

"They have found me!—those mean policemen, —they have found me!" she cried, and threw herself into the cupboard, the door of which Clarice had left open, who now in the greatest terror locked it, and concealed the key in the bosom of her dress.

A loud knock and ring at the hall-door followed immediately, and then two policemen, not waiting for the servant to obey the summons, came straight into the Library.

They were much surprised at seeing Clarice, who, when they entered, had presence of mind enough to return to the marble table, and busy herself assiduously with arranging the flowers in tall crystal vases. The roses looked exquisite, hanging over the cool, sparkling edges of the pretty cups; but Clarice, a moment before so engrossed with the mysteries of their existence, had no power now of even distinguishing one blossom from the other, or of judging how they should be placed. Her heart beat violently, and she felt as if the crisis of *her* fate—not Olga's—had come.

"Your servant, Miss," said the tall policeman, the results of whose vigilance had so greatly excited her father's suspicions. "Didn't guess you were here, Ma'am—don't wish to startle you; but where's the little varmint who scampered in here just now?"

"Little varmint?"

"Yes, Miss, the little varmint of a thief we're on the scent of. She's been hid in this here house three days—bless'd if she hasn't; but we've cotch'd her now. She came right in here, and no mistake—blow'd if she didn't! Where did she go, Miss?"

"You can see for yourself that there is nobody here," replied Clarice, astonished to find herself speaking, and speaking calmly too; but the unexpected strength was born from the emergency of the moment.

"Bless yer heart, Miss, we *saw* her race into this here room, and there's not another door from it, and the blinds outside the windows is closed, so she can't have left by any natural aperture." (Doors and windows were the policeman's idea of natural apertures.) "You mustn't evade the law, Miss—you mustn't, indeed. Where is she, please?"

"Papa will be angry at your coming here while he is out. He was not at all pleased at your searching the house last night, and he says he *knows* there is no one concealed in it."

"But you and I know better than that, Miss,"

replied the policeman, winking at her. "Just you show me where she is, and we'll go away as quiet as two blessed lambs—we will indeed!"

"But you must go away quietly at once," said poor Clarice, so dreadfully frightened that fear gave her what appeared to herself to be supernatural courage. "You will search the house at your peril without my consent—you have no warrant!"

The words "You have no warrant!" seemed to her to come from her lips, without her having summoned them, or intended to say them. Whether they sprang there from her recollection of what her father and Mr Linton had said, she really did not know.

"Well," said the policeman, "this here go—though an uncommon rum go—is of no manner of use. We've Hughes with us—the man who saw her in the wood—and he's identified her, and he'll swear to her—*he* will; and he's gone for Mr Herbert the magistrate—*he* has, and they'll be here immediate; and you'll not refuse a magistrate, I expect, even if he hadn't got no warrant."

"But meantime," said Clarice, tears bursting from her eyes, though she did not sob nor cry in an ordinary manner; "meantime you are very rude to come in here on a young lady like me. Be so good as to go into the servants' hall, and wait there till these other people come."

Only to get rid of them for five minutes! she thought—only that; and so to spirit Olga away to some other place—only that! I ask nothing more, I want nothing more—only to be rid of these men!

But the policeman put his tongue into his cheek. "Servant, Miss!" said he; "but this pig won't squeak. The thief's here in this room, and here in this room it's our *dooty* to stay till Mr Herbert comes."

"Please—please go away!" cried Clarice, changing her tone all in a minute to one of abject entreaty. "I've got five pounds of my own, and I'll give it you all if you'll only go away."

"Oh, come now, Miss! this won't do at any price. Don't you try to bribe me, please! it's punishable; and it only makes this difference, that if I just could have gone before, I just can't go now!"

Another thundering knock and ring at the hall-door, and Wilson ushered Mr Herbert into the apartment, accompanied by the man Hughes, who had seen Olga in the wood.

Clarice knew Mr Herbert very slightly, in the way in which girls of her age do know middle-aged gentlemen, who visit their parents. He shook hands with her kindly, and his first thought was for her, before he so much as looked at the policemen.

"This is very unpleasant for you, Miss Clavering—I am so sorry—and your father not at home too. Won't you go into another room and let us settle our business? Don't mind us—that's your best plan."

Clarice, in perfect silence, instantly turned to obey his advice, pressing the key against her as she did so, as a sign to herself of Olga's safety. "She *is* safe," thought she, "if only she does not begin to neigh!"

But the policeman stopped her, by placing himself, though in a very respectful manner, between her and the door.

"I think, Sir," said he, "the young lady hadn't better go. She was here when the thief came, she was; and she knows where the thief is, she does."

"Oh, that alters the case," replied Mr Herbert, cheerfully, "and where is she, then, my dear Miss Clavering?"

"He has no right to say such a thing," murmured Clarice.

"What!—were you not here?"

No answer.

"And don't you know where she is?"

Still no reply.

Mr Herbert looked first at Clarice, and then at the policeman, who, when he had met his glance, elevated his eyebrows very expressively, and shook his head.

"Why, what does it all mean?" asked the perplexed magistrate.

"The young lady has hid the kid," said the policeman at last, though with evident reluctance, "and offered me a five-pounder to go away."

Mr Herbert gave a little low whistle.

"But you know this is quite a mistake of yours," he said, turning to Clarice, and speaking in a kind, but peremptory manner; "it is very wrong—very wrong indeed, to try and defeat justice, and you may bring very unpleasant consequences on yourself and your father; you *must* tell where the girl is."

"I cannot," replied she, in a low hoarse voice.

"Do you mean that you don't know?"

Total silence.

"She *must* know," said the policeman; "the gal is a mad gal. She was on the roof of the house yesterday, and to-day we found her up a tree, and she ran for it, and got in here before we did, but we *seen* her whisk into this very room; for it's opposite the hall-door, and she was in too great fright to close *it* after her, and then Miss here ordered us out—and when we wouldn't go, offered me a five-pounder to make myself scarce—Miss did; and you see yourself, Sir, there's no way the gal can have crept out, only the one door she came in at, and we followed her close, and Miss *must* know where the gal is, she must."

"Well, Miss Clavering, I am very sorry," said the magistrate, "but if you won't give me the information, I must order the men to search the room."

"You have not got a warrant," cried Clarice, harping back on the words she had heard.

Mr Herbert looked both surprised and affronted.

"Oh, havn't I?" said he; "don't trouble yourself about that, pray. I'll make my conduct good to Mr Clavering when he comes home."

Ah, he will be here soon, thought she, and then matters will be even worse than they are now.

"Now, my men," said Mr Herbert, "look about you, and be smart. I don't want to annoy the young lady more than is actually necessary."

The men hunted through every place in which it would be possible to hide a fly, but in vain, and then came to a stand-still before the cupboard-door, wherein Olga lay concealed.

"Here she is," said they; "this is locked—she is in here."

"Are you sure?" said Mr Herbert, who knew that, under less self-evident circumstances, the instinct of policemen might be trusted.

"Certain sure," was the reply.

"Now, Miss Clavering, there is nothing left for it; you must give me the key of that door if you have it, or tell me where it is if you have not got it."

"I cannot," said Clarice, and felt as she spoke as if the world was coming to an end, and she had better die off quietly at once.

"Nonsense—you can, and you must."

"No—I will not give it to you."

"Do you know what you are about, young lady? Do you know that I can have you sent to prison for refusing?" said the magistrate, putting on a very stern face.

"I can't help it," was the breathless answer. "You must send me to prison if you choose, but I can't give you the key."

"And I really can't waste my time here all day," said Mr Herbert, impatiently.

Neither of the eager speakers knew that another person had entered the room, and was standing in the door-way listening to every word they said.

Mr Herbert turned to the policeman.

"Higgins," said he, "you go up to my house, and tell my man to give you the locked portfolio

in my office." Then to Clarice, frowning, and assuming a look of extreme severity, and speaking very sternly (poor Clarice had not the faintest idea that he was only trying to frighten her into giving up the key), "I have sent him on an errand from which he will return in ten minutes. I shall then make out a warrant to search the house, and unless you assist me as far as lies in your power, my duty will compel me to commit you to prison for harbouring a thief. I will give you that time for reflection. No," interrupting himself, as he perceived how white she grew; "I forgot—it is not necessary to wait. I have papers in my pocket." He took, or pretended to take, the required documents from his pocket, and sitting down at the writing table, dipped a pen in the ink. "Now, then, Miss Clavering, I am sorry to say that my duty will oblige me to commit you to prison, unless you give me the key. Now, then," with a portentous frown, and raising his voice, though speaking very slowly, "make up your mind—will you give up the key?—or will you go to prison?"

"I will go to prison," replied Clarice, in a low, sad, but resolved, voice.

"No, no, no!" cried bright, eager accents from within the cupboard, "you shan't—she shan't. Oh, horrid grown-up people! why won't you let children alone? Let me out—let me out—don't hurt my dear Clarice—she shan't go to prison—it's I ought to go, not she—only I hope my Papa will kill you. Let me out, Clarice—let me out!"

Mr Herbert looked utterly bewildered. Clarice began to cry, and the silent, unperceived listener at the door came hastily forward—a handsome soldierly-looking man in the prime of life, who took hold of both Clarice's hands and pressed them warmly within his. "It is my Olga," he said, with the air of a man accustomed to command; "let her out at once—nobody shall hurt her."

Clarice drew the key from her bosom, and Colonel Leslie—for, of course the stranger was no other than the Highland father of whom Olga was so proud—unlocked and opened the door of the cupboard.

Out tumbled little Olga, her golden hair all in a frizzy tangle, her cheeks flushed a brighter pink than the brightest of the July roses, and tears streaming from her heaven-blue eyes.

Her father caught her in his arms and kissed her repeatedly, but she only kept exclaiming, "Isn't she good? isn't she noble? isn't she grand? Oh, you dear Clarice—you dear good Clarice—you dear darling Clarice—you shan't go to prison—you shan't—you shan't!"

"No, no, no!" said Colonel Leslie, soothingly, "she shan't—of course she shan't. But oh, Olga, what have you been doing? how did you come here? and what does it all mean?"

"I suspect you are on a wrong scent, my men," said Mr Herbert, "and have brought me out on a fool's errand. This is a young lady, not a servant-girl."

"That's it," put in Olga. "I said it was so ridiculous advertising for me as a servant; it couldn't make me one, you know! And, Papa,

only fancy, they pretended I stole Aunt Annie's jewels!"

"But how did you come here, and what does it all mean?" repeated her perplexed and bewildered father. "I fear, Olga, you have been behaving very badly."

"No, indeed, Papa," said Olga, earnestly, "I have behaved quite goodly—I have, indeed. It's the old story," she continued, with a weary sigh, "all the grown-up people wrong, and the children to suffer. I ran away from school—yes, I did—but then, Papa, it was you put me there! a horrid bad school, Papa—why, even a clergyman said it was an injudicious school, and he would not advise a girl to go to it. Clarice told me so—even a clergyman, Papa! What could I do but run away? It was good of me—but then I'm a child, Papa, and children *are* good; and, as for Clarice, she's gooder than good and righter than right!" Here Olga's tears came pouring down her cheeks again, and, breaking from her father's arms, she ran up to Clarice, clasped her to her heart and kissed her passionately.

Meantime, Mr Herbert took the advertisement from his pocket-book and silently handed it to Colonel Leslie, who, receiving it with a polite but rather haughty bow, as silently read it. But, when he had finished its perusal, the colour mounted to his face, and he said, "What insolent folly!"

Then the much-enduring Wilson again came into the room, and, handing a letter to Mr Herbert, said, "A telegram for you, sir!"

Mr Herbert glanced at the contents. "This," said he, "is an answer to a telegram sent an hour ago to the address given in this advertisement, to say the"—he paused for an inoffensive word—"*person*, described in it, is found."

He then slowly read it aloud, in the way in which people do spell out telegrams:

On — a — wrong — scent —
She — is — already — here —

After which he looked round on everybody in the room, and just said, "So!"

"Of course," said Colonel Leslie, with some *hauteur* of manner; "of course, it never occurred to anybody that there was more than one school or one girl in the world; and that because Miss Leslie was so foolish as to run away, that did not make her either a servant or a thief."

Olga looked with admiring eyes at her father, nudged Clarice, and whispered, "Isn't he nice?" "Oh Papa!" added she aloud, "*why* didn't you come down in Highland costume? and I *told* you!"

Poor Hughes, who expected the reward, was quite crest-fallen, the police discomfited, and the magistrate put out. "I hope you will be a little more careful before you bring me a story again," said he, pointedly, and then dismissed them. "I see no reason why you should stay any longer in

Miss Clavering's drawing-room," he added, as if it gave him a pleasure to say something disagreeable to somebody.

"It's the Library," said Olga.

Mr Herbert made her a profound bow, to which she replied by a pretty little curtsey. "I must apologise both to Colonel Leslie and Miss Clavering," he said, "for these very unpleasant circumstances, but I really only did my duty."

"And I beg your pardon for my obstinacy, Mr Herbert," said Clarice, smiling through the tears that still kept springing to her eyes, "but I *could* not betray her."

"You behaved like a heroine, Miss Clavering," he replied gravely; "and of course you knew I was only trying to frighten you into giving up the key. Of course, I had not the slightest idea of really sending you to prison."

"Oh, you story-teller!" cried Olga, "and you spoke in such a nasty voice. Please couldn't you go away now? You're not wanted here any more than the policemen, are you? and it would be so *much* nicer if you were not here."

"Hush, Olga," said her father.

Mr Herbert winced a little, but he pretended not to mind, and took the hint in good part; so he did not hurry away as if he was affronted, but left soon enough to make Olga clap her hands and say, "Well, I suppose after all there always is some good even in the worst people. He *is* a villain though; isn't he, Papa? and to think of his telling such stories! Why, if he'd been a child he'd have been whipped for it; and he told of himself, and wasn't one bit ashamed." And then she kissed Clarice and said, "Oh Clarice, I shall be *such* a dull girl for ever after this—for I shall *never* do anything you bid me not!"

There was a great deal to explain to Colonel Leslie, and Olga's explanations were not always the most lucid; but Clarice came to the rescue, and gave a little help whenever she saw the hearer was becoming involved in hopeless perplexity; so that by degrees he began to understand all that had happened. He was both displeased and shocked, though Olga did her best to prevent his scolding her.

"No, Papa—not the first day—not when you've just come back—don't be cruel, Papa—I'd rather be advertised for than scolded," she said, when he attempted it.

He thanked Clarice for all her kindness, and paid his tribute to her heroism. "But," he added, "you must, I am sure, see that you ought to have told your father in the very first instance, without agreeing to conceal this naughty child at all; and, had you done so, all that has followed would have been avoided."

"You had *much* better advertise for me at once," pouted Olga, "than scold dear Clarice and call me naughty on the first day."

But Clarice, with eager candour, acknowledged her fault, and owned that she still dreaded to make the mystery of her conduct known to her father.

"I will beg you off," said Colonel Leslie; but this was not so easy a matter as he anticipated. Mr Clavering was extremely astonished at all that he heard on his return home, and extremely displeased also, which displeasure he visited on Clarice's head by very severe reproofs, to which she patiently submitted, as her conscience told her she deserved them. In the midst of them, Olga suddenly fainted away. The excitement and strain on the nerves had been too much for her, and she suffered also from the long confinement in the small, badly-ventilated cupboard. In fact, the two young ladies having done wrong, had to endure the penalty of their wrong-doing. Olga was really ill for some time; her meeting with her mother was clouded by anxiety and distress, and the kind-hearted, though thoughtless child, also felt keenly that by her folly her beloved Clarice was involved in disgrace. Clarice, on her part, grieved for Olga's illness, which she knew would have been avoided had she behaved as she ought to have done; and she grieved also for her father's displeasure, which did not abate either soon or easily. He had, however, taken a great fancy to Colonel Leslie, and though blaming Olga, was quite captivated by her, especially when he heard that it was she who had neighed in the closet. "If *I* had neighed in a closet he would have judged it differently," thought Clarice, rather bitterly, but she checked the thought, for she knew her father was not unjust to her, and that she had merited his displeasure.

At last Olga recovered, and at last Clarice was forgiven, and yielding to the earnest entreaties of everybody, Mr Clavering consented to take Clarice to spend that happy autumn at Glenkeen Castle. The vivid delight that a first visit to the Highlands must afford to a romantic and ardent young creature like Clarice need not be dwelt on here. The only drawback, perhaps, being the difference presented by the personal appearance of the two Papas when they went out shooting together, with dogs and guns. She saw Colonel Leslie dressed in Highland costume, and survived the sight—though it is not to be denied that she sometimes afterwards cast furtive sorrowful glances at her father's legs.

THE END

AFTERWORDS

****

Elizabeth Anna Hart, the author of *The Runaway* (1872) was the youngest of the four children of the Reverend Edward Smedley (1788–1836) and his wife Mary Hume, a reputedly 'intelligent, loving and forceful' woman whose sister Lucy was to be the grandmother of Lewis Carroll. At the time of Elizabeth's birth in 1822 her father preached at St James Chapel, Tottenham Court Road, and at St Giles, Camberwell; he wrote poetry, and essays for the British Critic, edited the Encyclopaedia Metropolitana, tutored young boy students until severely impaired hearing prevented this, and educated his own children, for example he taught his daughters Latin.

Some of the Rev. Smedley's letters were used by a friend in a memoir and from these we have a glimpse of the delightful nature of his home life. After the family moved to Dulwich he wrote in 1830:

> . . . You will perceive by my having proceeded thus far without a notice of the darlings, that they are most favourably convalescing. Elizabeth is still very delicate, but she is much brisker than ever this morning, and has just beaten, kicked and pinched me to my heart's

****

> delight. The thousand gentle and affectionate things which she has said and done will astonish you as they steal out by degrees. One morning, when I was going to town, I asked what I should bring her. She put up her hand and patted my cheek and said 'You' . . . But all this is fitter for others than for me . . .

This devoted father died at only forty-eight, when his youngest daughters, Menella and Elizabeth, were only eighteen and sixteen, and was never to know of their literary successes. Menella, inheriting his ill health, spent long periods in Tenby in Wales; as Menella Bute Smedley she published short stories, poems, several novels, and important articles on the education of girls and of pauper children. Her writing was often on a heroic or historical theme, entirely competent, skilfully crafted but, especially in her writing for children, lacking the sparkle and attractive absurdity of her sister Elizabeth's.

Meanwhile, in 1848, Elizabeth married Thomas Barnard Hart of Glen Alla, Donegal. He had been an officer in the Indian Army and was eighteen years her senior; there were no children. She wrote prolifically during her marriage and some of her books are set in Ireland, with amusing attempts at dialect; Glen Alla church and rectory were built by her partly from the proceeds of her books. However, her work for adults is forgotten and it was her cousin, Francis Smedley, a minor novelist and author of an early school classic, *Frank Farleigh* (1850), who achieved a place in the *Dictonary of National Biography*. Of all the Smedley books *The Runaway* is the only one that has survived – and that due to Gwen Raverat's love of it and desire to illustrate it.

I found some of her adult novels in the London Library and felt rather like a Victorian lady as I wallowed in *Freda* (1878, three volumes) and *Wilfred's Widow* (1883, two), with their stereotypical characters, complicated plots of deceptions, misdoings and mistaken identities and unbelievably rapid unwindings. Yet, I must admit, my interest was held, and I had to read to the happy endings.

One of her titles, *Miss Hitchcock's Wedding Dress* (1876), is a potentially witty idea which almost comes off. Miranda and her older sister Sophy, once wealthy but now earning their living as dressmakers, have been stitching, laboriously, at a wedding dress. One day Miranda cannot resist trying it on. Enranced by her own image in the looking-glass she runs impetuously out into the street, and joins the guests attending a grand party next door. Inevitably:

> A tall, very good-looking man, who had been watching her for some moments, though she was not in the least aware that he had been doing so, offered her his arm, saying, 'May I have the pleasure?' and she found herself in the next room before she knew where she was . . .

It is a 'Cinderella' story of some charm, although lacking the freshness of *The Runaway*.

Elizabeth's first success as a writer was with *Mrs Jerningham's Journal* (1869), a fast-moving and immensely readable novel in

****

verse about the newly married Mrs Jerningham, who is already filled with disquiet about what she has done.

> Why did they make me marry him?
> Life *was* so bright and *is* so dim!
> I cannot understand why men
> Should stop their growth at five feet ten;
> I meant my husband to be tall –
> Short men have such a shabby look –
> And then his nose is rather small,
> Without a notion of a hook.
>
> I wish he was a barrister,
> Then he could talk and cause a stir,
> And wear a lovely curly wig,
> To make his face look brown and big;
> A captain in a uniform
> Might take a woman's heart by storm;
> And sailors are the best of all,
> Such charming partners at a ball:
> But just a banker – don't you see,
> It is so very tame and flat –
> Why *did* he want to marry me?
> How *could* Papa consent to that?

(Mrs Jerningham is as passionate and outspoken as Olga in *The Runaway*, who also likes men in uniform; could it have been the Indian Army uniform that persuaded Elizabeth to marry?) *Mrs Jerningham's Journal* received glowing reviews on publication, the *Edinburgh Daily Review* writing: 'It is a nearly perfect gem . . . we have had few things so good for a long time, and those who neglect to read it, are neglecting one of the jewels of contemporary literature.'

In the same year, 1869, Elizabeth and her sister published *Child-World*, their second book of poems for children, the first being *Poems Written for a Child* (1868). This was glowingly praised by the *Saturday Review*, which especially praised the authors' 'privilege of innocence, to discern what is hidden from older and more world-worn eyes and hearts.' Although Menella's poetry can be found in collections of Victorian women's poetry, and some of Elizabeth's survives in twentieth century anthologies, more would be worth reviving. This is especially so of some of Elizabeth's strange narratives, since she was essentially a storyteller. Here is the first verse of the rather bizarre 'Ogres':

> 'Bring me a child!' said the Ogre,
> 'Bring me a child to eat;
> And let it be a lively one,
> And very fair and sweet!
> A flaxen-headed creature,
> And, oh, it must be fat;
> Bring me a child – a naughty child!'
> The Ogre said, and sat.

Many of Elizabeth's poems suggest a vivid imagination and yield some funny and fantastic ideas, bordering on nonsense. Rudyard Kipling recalled her *Child-Nature* (1869) when writing about his childhood reading in 1935: he remembered a book 'full of lovely tales in strange metres. A girl was turned into a water-rat "as a matter of course"; an Urchin cured an old man of gout by means of a cool cabbage-leaf, and somehow "forty wicked Goblins" were mixed up in the plot; and a "Darling" got out on the house-leads with a broom and tried to sweep stars off the skies.' As Roger Lancelyn Green wrote in *Tellers of Tales* in 1946: 'Mrs Hart at her best shows a breath-takingly vivid insight and understanding of child-nature and a captivating power of narration in the simple and most fluent verse of poems both tender and fantastic, straight from the genuine and perennial heart of childhood.'

In the sixteen years between publication of *The Runaway* and Elizabeth Anna Hart's death her output was startling, consisting of some fourteen titles. *Harry*, written in 1877, the year of Menella's death, is an obvious attempt to follow up the considerable success of *Mrs Jerningham's Journal*, but remains a poor relation. A rather turgid, melodramatic verse-novel, it is more on the lines of *John Jerningham's Journal*, published in America in 1876 and author unknown.

It is the children's books that are engaging, moving and funny. Among many still readable titles *May Cunningham's Trials* (1883) and *Daisy's Dilemma* (1888) stand out, with their outspoken, mischievous, often misunderstood child characters, and lively dialogue between boys and girls. A poem in *Child-Nature* is called 'Little Girls' and begins:

What can little girls do,
  Even if they would?

****

Oh, if we were grown-up men,
  Wouldn't we be good!
Wouldn't we kill dragons?
  Wouldn't we make laws?
Nobody should run in debt –
  No one lose a cause.
We would turn the prisons
  Into houses grand,
Where the poor should eat and drink
  Till they could not stand.

It ends: 'What can little girls do,/Even if they would?/Oh, if we were grown-up men,/*Wouldn't* we be good!' This is an echo of Olga's outburst in *The Runaway*: '"Oh, yes, *boys* . . . but then boys are so *much* better than girls, and boys do become their own masters very often while they are still boys – hardly older, you know, than you and I are. It's girls that are kept under and kept down; and so there's nothing left for girls but to run away, just as I did; and it would be hard to blame a poor creature for that.'

Despite these feminist sentiments few have now heard of Elizabeth Anna Hart and it is only Menella who is mentioned in recent feminist companions to English literature. But the novelist Charlotte Yonge (whose 1862 *Countess Kate* may well have influenced *The Runaway*) admired her work and wrote approvingly that 'exceedingly droll mishaps befall the little maid who hides the runaway from school in her cupboard.' Roger Lancelyn Green called her 'the elusive Mrs Elizabeth Anna Hart', describing *The Runaway* as 'her most completely

****

successful book because of its admirable plot' and 'a brilliant and undeservedly forgotten foretaste of the understanding of childhood which was so near . . . Mrs Hart's great gift lies in her understanding of the child-mind and outlook – the universal child and not to any particular degree the young Victorian miss. Genuine child-thoughts and child-imaginings simply bubble from the lips of her juvenile characters, and a wonderful gaiety and lightness of touch runs through all her books for the young.'

Anne Harvey, 2002

****

One day in 1935 the publishing house Macmillan received a letter from the wood-engraver Gwen Raverat: would they consider republishing Elizabeth Anna Hart's 1872 novel *The Runaway*, with illustrations by herself? She wrote persuasively, recommending it as 'a gay, rather farcical book, which was the delight of my own childhood (and I suppose of the generation before as well) and has been very much loved by my own children, and by many others.' Then too, she added: 'The book is short, very amusing; not a tear or a prayer in it; I believe it might have some success; and it would be amusing to illustrate it with pictures in the dresses of the [eighteen] sixties.' This recommendation suggests that Gwen Raverat had little patience with the desire, often found among Victorian children's writers, to mould, educate and improve – a habit that often worked against the simultaneous need to intrigue and enchant.

She had come across *The Runaway* as a child at Down House, the home of her Darwin grandparents, and knew well that the book offers unalloyed pleasure. It had first been published by Macmillan in 1872, seven years after they had brought out the first edition of Lewis Carroll's *Alice's Adventures in Wonderland*. For, although this firm is associated with Hardy, Arnold, Tennyson and Yeats, it also had a flair for children's books, catching a number of best-sellers, among them the two Alice books, Thomas Hughes's *Tom Brown's Schooldays* and Charles Kingsley's *The Water-Babies*.

Gwen Raverat's letter did not go unheeded: Macmillan's expressed immediate interest, for her illustrations, both drawn and engraved, were much in demand by commercial publishers. She had in fact helped pioneer the wood-engraving revival which flourished between the wars, and exhibited regularly with the Society of Wood-Engravers, of which she was a founder-member. Immediately before turning her attention to *The Runaway* she had worked on three of her finest illustrated books: *The Cambridge Book of Poetry for Children*, Frances Cornford's *Mountains and Molehills* and *Four Tales from Hans Andersen*. All three make use of wood-engravings and had been produced by Cambridge University Press, where Gwen Raverat had good relations with the printers. She was eager to build on the experience she had acquired: in the agreement reached with Macmillan, she not only requested a say in the size of page and choice of type, but also made it a condition that *The Runaway* should be printed in Cambridge at the University Press. 'They are used to printing from wood blocks, which is a great advantage as far as I am concerned; & are most excellent printers, & are no dearer than other printers I think.'

One reason why wood-engraving makes such a good medium for book illustration is that it can be locked in the chase with the type and printed in one fell swoop. Cut in to the end grain of the wood, it is necessarily a severe and disciplined medium, also very satisfactory in the way that the taut, crisp results, with their sparkling rich interplay of blacks and whites, can balance the weight and density of the text. Gwen Raverat, an expert in this field, exploits this cleverly in *The Runaway*, her designs filling the pages in a variety of ways: they punctuate each new chapter with headings; infiltrate single figures every time a new character is introduced; occasionally slice unexpectedly at an angle across the page, or unfold in a double-page spread. And she achieved an even more satisfying balance between text and image than in her previous books by changing from Bodoni to Scotch Roman, a larger, more modern typeface. Text and illustrations transmute this charming, lively tale into a small work of art – with the result that the 1936 edition of *The Runaway* has become less a children's book than a collector's item.

Initially Gwen Raverat had turned to wood-engraving as a stand-alone art form, teaching herself, while a student at the Slade School of Art, how to hold the various tools, how to turn the boxwood block as it rests on the sandbag in order to achieve a curved line, all the while patiently cutting away those parts that would appear white in the final print. As the image develops, the gradual progression from darkness to light often gives the maker the sensation of something growing ever brighter in one's hands.

Later, after Gwen Raverat moved into the Old Rectory at Harlton, outside Cambridge, where she did the illustrations for *The Runaway*, she would work at a table near the window in the main living-room, in the company of her two daughters and their friends. She always sat facing the garden, with her back to the room and could seem, with her slightly humped figure, wholly absorbed in her task; but every now and then would join in the conversation or suddenly turn round and look searchingly at the speaker through her dark-rimmed glasses. At night time she worked by the light of an acetylane lamp, in front of which stood the traditional resource for engravers – a glass globe filled with water, which, when placed between the lamp and the worker protected the face and hands from the heat of the lamp. The white flame of the acetylane lamp, transmuted through this glass globe, created a clear, cool light. It fell on the blocks of polished boxwood and the surrounding tools – gravers, tint-tool, gouger, spitz-sticker or scooper – with which Gwen Raverat steadily excavated her imaginary figures, interiors, garden scenes or landscapes, until they reached completion and became instinct with feeling and sharpness of vision.

With *The Runaway* she felt very much at home in the Victorian world it represented, with its crinoline dresses and its enormous four-poster beds. The latter took her back in memory to Down House, where the beds had 'ceilings and curtains of stiff shiny chintz hanging all round them,' as she recollects in her account of her childhood, *Period Piece*. Here, too, we find that dry humour which she enjoyed in *The Runaway*.

Her interpretation of the story uncovers a generosity in the scale of things: the headpiece to Chapter II, showing Clarice taking tea with her father, amply conveys a sense of mid-Victorian comfort. Each vignette in the novel, either inset or used as a headpiece or tailpiece, offers an imaginative insight and deepens the reader's involvement with the story. But it is the handling of light that makes many of these sixty illustrations so deft and poignant, as it pours across curtains, round figures and over table tops; it is also a source of tenderness, betraying the artist's love for the tale, for Clarice and Olga, and the tension created by their drama.

The 1936 edition of *The Runaway* went out of print after six years. In 1946 Gwen Raverat was surprised to hear it being read on Children's Hour on the radio and she wrote to Macmillan, asking if it could be reprinted. Nothing happened, but a few years later she persuaded Duckworth to republish the book, which they did in 1953, Macmillan agreeing to relinquish all rights to her illustrations. It seems that the book remained dear to heart, having been shaped in part in her mind by her imagination. Without any doubt, this new edition, published some sixty-five years after her illustrations were first produced, would have greatly pleased her.

Frances Spalding
London, 2002

Olga's Grandmamma, who fumbled her fingers.

Ann, who thought she saw a ghost.

Wilson, the butler who wondered why Clarice ate so much.

The real Mrs Jennings, who kept a school in Yorkshire.

Olga, who was afraid in the cupboard.

Dr Smith, who came to see Miss Simmonds.

Aunt Jessie, who wouldn't do at all.

Mr Linton, the Rector, who found Olga's letter.

Clarice, who told Olga to be careful while she was out.

The false Mrs Jennings.

If you have enjoyed this Persephone book why not telephone or write to us for a free copy of the Persephone Catalogue and the current Persephone Biannually? All Persephone books ordered from us cost £10 or three for £27 plus £2 postage per book.

PERSEPHONE BOOKS LTD
59 Lamb's Conduit Street
London WC1N 3NB

Telephone: 020 7242 9292
Fax: 020 7242 9272
sales@persephonebooks.co.uk
www.persephonebooks.co.uk

Persephone Books publishes forgotten fiction and non-fiction by unjustly neglected authors. The following titles are available:

No. 1 *William – an Englishman* (1919) by Cicely Hamilton
No. 2 *Mariana* (1940) by Monica Dickens
No. 3 *Someone at a Distance* (1953) by Dorothy Whipple
No. 4 *Fidelity* (1915) by Susan Glaspell
No. 5 *An Interrupted Life: the Diaries and Letters of Etty Hillesum 1941–43*
No. 6 *The Victorian Chaise-longue* (1953) by Marghanita Laski
No. 7 *The Home-Maker* (1924) by Dorothy Canfield Fisher
No. 8 *Good Evening, Mrs. Craven: the Wartime Stories of Mollie Panter-Downes 1939–44*
No. 9 *Few Eggs and No Oranges: the Diaries of Vere Hodgson 1940–45*
No. 10 *Good Things in England* (1932) by Florence White
No. 11 *Julian Grenfell* (1976) by Nicholas Mosley
No. 12 *It's Hard to be Hip over Thirty and Other Tragedies of Married Life* (1968) by Judith Viorst
No. 13 *Consequences* (1919) by E. M. Delafield
No. 14 *Farewell Leicester Square* (1941) by Betty Miller
No. 15 *Tell It to a Stranger: Stories from the 1940s* by Elizabeth Berridge
No. 16 *Saplings* (1945) by Noel Streatfeild
No. 17 *Marjory Fleming* (1946) by Oriel Malet
No. 18 *Every Eye* (1956) by Isobel English
No. 19 *They Knew Mr. Knight* (1934) by Dorothy Whipple
No. 20 *A Woman's Place: 1910–1975* by Ruth Adam
No. 21 *Miss Pettigrew Lives for a Day* (1938) by Winifred Watson
No. 22 *Consider the Years 1938–1946* by Virginia Graham
No. 23 *Reuben Sachs* (1888) by Amy Levy
No. 24 *Family Roundabout* (1948) by Richmal Crompton
No. 25 *The Montana Stories* (1921) by Katherine Mansfield
No. 26 *Brook Evans* (1928) by Susan Glaspell

No. 27 *The Children Who Lived in a Barn* (1938) by Eleanor Graham
No. 28 *Little Boy Lost* (1949) by Marghanita Laski
No. 29 *The Making of a Marchioness* (1901) by Frances Hodgson Burnett
No. 30 *Kitchen Essays* (1922) by Agnes Jekyll
No. 31 *A House in the Country* (1944) by Jocelyn Playfair
No. 32 *The Carlyles at Home* (1965) by Thea Holme
No. 33 *The Far Cry* (1949) by Emma Smith
No. 34 *Minnie's Room: the Peacetime Stories of Mollie Panter-Downes 1947–65*
No. 35 *Greenery Street* (1925) by Denis Mackail
No. 36 *Lettice Delmer* (1958) by Susan Miles
No. 37 *The Runaway* (1872) by Elizabeth Anna Hart
No. 38 *Cheerful Weather for the Wedding* (1932) by Julia Strachey
No. 39 *Manja* (1939) by Anna Gmeyner
No. 40 *The Priory* (1939) by Dorothy Whipple
No. 41 *Hostages to Fortune* (1933) by Elizabeth Cambridge
No. 42 *The Blank Wall* (1947) by Elisabeth Sanxay Holding
No. 43 *The Wise Virgins* (1914) by Leonard Woolf
No. 44 *Tea with Mr Rochester* (1949) by Frances Towers
No. 45 *Good Food on the Aga* (1933) by Ambrose Heath
No. 46 *Miss Ranskill Comes Home* (1946) by Barbara Euphan Todd
No. 47 *The New House* (1936) by Lettice Cooper
No. 48 *The Casino* (1948) by Margaret Bonham
No. 49 *Bricks and Mortar* (1932) by Helen Ashton
No. 50 *The World that was Ours* (1967) by Hilda Bernstein
No. 51 *Operation Heartbreak* (1950) by Duff Cooper
No. 52 *The Village* (1952) by Marghanita Laski
No. 53 *Lady Rose and Mrs Memmary* (1937) by Ruby Ferguson
No. 54 *They Can't Ration These* (1940) by Vicomte de Mauduit
No. 55 *Flush* (1933) by Virginia Woolf
No. 56 *They Were Sisters* (1943) by Dorothy Whipple
No. 57 *The Hopkins Manuscript* (1939) by R C Sherriff
No. 58 *Hetty Dorval* (1947) by Ethel Wilson

No. 59 *There Were No Windows* (1944) by Norah Hoult
No. 60 *Doreen* (1946) by Barbara Noble
No. 61 *A London Child of the 1870s* (1934) by Molly Hughes
No. 62 *How to Run your Home without Help* (1949) by Kay Smallshaw
No. 63 *Princes in the Land* (1938) by Joanna Cannan
No. 64 *The Woman Novelist and Other Stories* (1946) by Diana Gardner
No. 65 *Alas, Poor Lady* (1937) by Rachel Ferguson
No. 66 *Gardener's Nightcap* (1938) by Muriel Stuart
No. 67 *The Fortnight in September* (1931) by RC Sherriff
No. 68 *The Expendable Man* (1963) by Dorothy B Hughes
No. 69 *Journal of Katherine Mansfield* (1927)
No. 70 *Plats du Jour* (1957) by Patience Gray and Primrose Boyd
No. 71 *The Shuttle* (1907) by Frances Hodgson Burnett
No. 72 *House-Bound* (1942) by Winifred Peck
No. 73 *The Young Pretenders* (1895) by Edith Henrietta Fowler
No. 74 *The Closed Door and Other Stories* by Dorothy Whipple
No. 75 *On the Other Side: Letters to my Children from Germany 1940–46* by Mathilde Wolff-Mönckeberg
No. 76 *The Crowded Street* (1924) by Winifred Holtby
No. 77 *Daddy's Gone A-Hunting* (1958) by Penelope Mortimer
No. 78 *A Very Great Profession: The Woman's Novel 1914–39* (1983) by Nicola Beauman
No. 79 *Round about a Pound a Week* (1913) by Maud Pember Reeves
No. 80 *The Country Housewife's Book* (1934) by Lucy H Yates
No. 81 *Miss Buncle's Book* (1934) by DE Stevenson
No. 82 *Amours de Voyage* (1849) by Arthur Hugh Clough
No. 83 *Making Conversation* (1931) by Christine Longford
No. 84 *A New System of Domestic Cookery* (1806) by Mrs Rundell
No. 85 *High Wages* (1930) by Dorothy Whipple
No. 86 *To Bed with Grand Music* (1946) by 'Sarah Russell' (Marghanita Laski)